SENSE OF PLACE

THE THOMAS ELKIN SERIES : BOOK THREE

N.R. WALKER

COPYRIGHT

BLURB

Book three in the Thomas Elkin series

Designing homes is easy. Finding home is something else entirely.

Thomas Elkin and Cooper Jones finally have the support of their families, and their love grows stronger every day. Now living together, they think nothing can stand in their way.

But there are outside influences trying to pull them apart.

Cooper encounters a man, closer to his age and with connections high up the property development chain, who wants Cooper as his own. Tom encounters discrimination and a hidden agenda from a fellow senior partner who's trying to take him down.

No matter what the world throws at them, Tom and Cooper are the real deal. Age differences aside, Tom has finally found his sense of place. His one true center, his home.

DEDICATION

For my husband...

SENSE OF PLACE

N.R. WALKER

CHAPTER ONE

Definition: Sense of place—a quality of design where the building and/or space achieves a sensory, emotional and spiritual connection to the site in which it is placed.

Source: Architecturewiki

I DID up the last of the buttons on my shirt, and my doctor sat down in his chair behind his desk. "Well, Tom, your blood pressure is fine, and"—he looked down at the piece of paper in the file—"all test results came back clear. Cholesterol is good, blood glucose is fine, STDs all clear, PSA is good."

I nodded and sat down across from him. "And everything else looks okay?"

He double-checked the papers in front of him. "I have

to say, you're the healthiest I've ever seen you. What's your secret?"

"Um..."

The doctor smiled. "Who is he?"

I let out an embarrassed laugh. "He's, um... he's a lot younger than me."

My doctor smiled and nodded, knowingly. "Well, whatever he's doing is working. I know you're concerned about your health, with the passing of your father, and that's completely understandable. But, Tom," he said, "I'd say you're a picture of health. Diet and exercise looks good on you."

"I need to work out, just to keep up with him," I admitted.

The doctor laughed at that. Then his smile faded. "Do you practice safe sex with your partner?"

"Yes, of course."

"How long have you been together?"

"About six months."

"Are you exclusive?"

"Yes. We live together." Then I added, "Well, that's kind of new. He moved in with me two weeks ago."

My doctor tilted his head. "Will you be looking to have unprotected sex with him?"

I hadn't even considered the idea. "Um, no...," I started. "Well, maybe... I'm not sure. We've not discussed that."

"When was he last tested?"

"Um—" Shit, I had to think about that. "He was tested just before he moved here. He's only been with me since."

"Anyway," he said casually, "if you do decide it's something you want to explore, then I'll be more than happy to run the necessary tests for him too."

I shook my head, a little daunted by the concept. "Okay."

"Don't feel you *have* to have unprotected sex, Tom," he went on to say. "A lot of gay couples don't, a lot do. It's something you need to discuss with your partner."

I left the doctor's appointment probably more conflicted than when I'd arrived. It had been a late appointment, and when I got home, Cooper was cooking dinner. Well, he was making a mess—dinner, not so much.

"Oh, hey," he said with a smile, looking up from the stove. "Working late?"

"No," I said, putting my briefcase on the table. "Doctor's appointment."

Cooper looked up at me, alarmed. "Everything okay?"

"Yeah." I gave him a kiss on the cheek. "Everything's fine. Just got the test results from my full checkup."

Cooper still looked concerned. "You sure you're okay?"

I gave him a bit of a nod and a shrug. "It's just with the way Dad died," I said. "I think I need to keep an eye on my health."

Cooper frowned and his eyebrows furrowed. He stopped stirring a pan of sauce and put the spoon down. "Tom, please don't talk like that."

I cupped his face in my hands and kissed him. "Cooper, sweetheart, no one expected my dad to have a stroke. I'd be foolish not to take that on board."

"I just can't think about you like that," he said quietly. "I can't even begin..."

"Hey." I kissed him again. "My doctor actually said I'm the fittest he's seen me. I told him I can credit you for that."

He smiled then. "He said you were okay?"

"A picture of health."

His eyes widened. "What tests did you have?"

"The usual," I answered. "Cholesterol, blood sugar, HIV, PSA..."

"What's PSA?"

"Prostate test."

"Prostate?" Cooper asked, looking a little miffed. "I hope he bought you dinner first."

I snorted out a laugh. "It's a standard lab test these days."

"Oh," he said, seemingly disappointed. "That's a shame."

Smiling, I looked around at the kitchen counter. "What are we eating?"

"It's supposed to be poached chicken," he said, turning back to the stove. "Well, it will be if I can get it cooked. And there's a mango dressing to go on it, but I haven't got to that yet."

"Where did you learn to cook this?"

"I called my mom for the recipe," he said with a grin.

"Can I do anything to help?"

"Yeah, you could cut up the mango and add all the dressing stuff," he said. "There's a recipe here somewhere."

I smiled as I scoured through the mess on the counter until I found the piece of paper with a handwritten recipe. I cleared a space, cleaning up what I could, and set about doing my task.

"Oh," I said as nonchalantly as I could. "My doctor said he'll add you to his list of patients if you wanted to go to him to have any tests done."

He looked thoughtful as he turned the chicken. "Mmm, I'm about due to be tested again."

I slid the diced mango into a mixing dish. "I know it's not exactly pleasant dinner conversation, and the fact we have to have tests done at all is an awful reality, but it's something we should talk about."

Cooper shrugged indifferently. "No, it's not that," he said. "I was just hoping to find a doctor who did prostate exams the old-fashioned way."

I laughed at him, and he smirked as he put the cooked chicken on a plate. I squeezed some lemon over the mango, and told him, "I can check your prostate for you later, if you'd like."

He slid in beside me and playfully bit my shoulder. "Do you want me to call you doctor?"

I kissed his cheek. "No, Tom is fine." I took a clean board and chopped red peppers. He threw in some type of canned bean, stirred it all together, and spooned it over the chicken.

It was pretty freakin' good.

"This was beautiful," I told him. "How come you don't cook more often?"

"Did you like it?" he asked excitedly. "My mom makes it all the time."

"We eat a lot of takeout," I mused out loud.

"You can cook tomorrow night. I think we should have grilled Thai fish with a bean shoot salad."

I chuckled at him. "I think you overestimate my cooking ability."

Cooper stood up, took my plate, and walked into the kitchen. "Just as well you're good in bed."

Smiling, I cleared the table and followed him into the kitchen where I kissed the back of his neck. "I'll clean up. You start the work you brought home."

When I had the kitchen back to spotless, I pulled out my laptop and a job file and set up my own workspace across from Cooper.

He was engrossed in his work. His head was down, looking from his laptop to the file in front of him and back again, and there was that concentration line between his eyebrows which meant he was trying to get his thoughts around something.

I opened my job file and flipped open my laptop, but I just couldn't get started. My mind was elsewhere.

"You okay?" Cooper asked.

I looked at him then, not even aware I'd zoned out. "Um, sure. Just not really in the mood for work tonight."

"Oh...," he said, then he looked at his own work. "I can pack this up if you'd prefer."

I laughed. "No, keep at it. You look engrossed in whatever it is you're doing."

Cooper sighed. "Actually, I'm stuck on something. Can I pick your brain?"

"Sure," I said, brightening. "Of course you can."

"Well." His brow furrowed. "We've just signed with a developer who I met with at the Philly energy convention. He wants to incorporate the design concepts in a commercial refit. He has a list of requirements and I'm not sure they'll work."

"How so?"

Cooper launched into how the existing building structure was confined by New York building restrictions, and how the desired energy compliance wasn't feasible without some external façade changes, and how he had to find a middle ground. "He really liked the glazing concept that I used on the Philly design, but I can't use that if I keep with the façade guidelines for the Riverdale district."

"Can I have a look at it?" I asked.

"Please do." He pushed his laptop out a little.

I pulled my seat around to his, and for the next hour

and a half, we went over the plans, job specifications, and New York City building codes. It was fascinating how his ideas differed from mine. His were new and exciting whereas mine were traditional and tested.

"I can bring home some old job sheets from work," I said. "I've done work in this district, so I can see what building permits we needed. You might be able to find a loophole."

"Would you?" he asked. "That'd be great! I mean, I don't want you to get into trouble."

"It's not privy information," I told him. "Anyone could check city records, but this will just save time. Is the original structure pre- or post-1940?"

"Pre."

"I'll check our records with the Preservation Commission," I offered. Then I smiled. "I'm sure you can figure out a way to make the new and old coexist."

"Yes, between us we have the whole retrofit thing covered, don't we?" he said with a nod. "You know, me being modern, you being antique."

I rolled my eyes at him. "At least I'm post-1940."

"Just as well," he said with a laugh. "Because I didn't get a permit from the Preservation Commission to date you."

"You're such a little shit," I said, grabbing his chin between my thumb and forefinger and planting a kiss on his lips. "I offer to help and you insult me."

Cooper grinned and stood up, only to straddle me in the seat. "You're so sexy when you try to act all hurt."

"Sexy, huh?" I asked with a smile. "Now you're just trying to sweet-talk me."

He leaned down and kissed me, pulling my bottom lip between his. Then he whispered gruffly, "You have no idea how sexy you are."

I looked into his darkening eyes. "I could say the same about you."

He kissed me again, rocking his hips on mine. "You promised me a physical examination."

"Then I best make it thorough."

He grinned, and I kissed him, then I stood us up and walked him backward to the bedroom, never taking my mouth from his.

He wanted me to check his prostate. So I did.

Twice.

I walked into my office on Monday morning and smiled at my personal assistant. "Morning, Jennifer."

"Good morning, Mr. Elkin," she replied professionally. "I trust you and Mr. Jones had a good weekend."

"Yes, we did," I answered, flipping through my messages. We'd gone out on Friday night for a few drinks. Cooper had spent the weekend going over the old files I'd brought home for him while I did some work, but mostly I'd annoyed him. We'd worked out; we'd cooked lunch and dinner both days. "It was lovely, thank you. And how was yours?"

"Very well, thank you," she replied. "You're early today. If you'd like, I can bring in fresh coffee."

"That'd be great," I told her.

Barely two minutes later, Jennifer carried in my coffee. But she frowned. "Were you expecting a meeting with Robert?"

Robert Chandler was one of the other senior partners

here. He'd mentored me, and even though I was on an equal footing as a senior partner, I'd always thought of him as a boss. He'd even gone with Jennifer to my father's funeral just four weeks ago.

"No, I wasn't expecting a meeting, why?"

"He's asked to see you," she said.

"Oh, okay."

"Did something happen between you?" she asked, rather cryptically.

"No. Why do you ask?"

Jennifer wasn't displaying her usual cool demeanor. She even seemed concerned. "Well, he asked to see you *now*. Told me to hold all calls, and asked that you see him first. He didn't exactly seem happy about it."

CHAPTER TWO

GRACE, Robert's personal assistant, opened the double doors for me and announced my expected arrival.

"Robert, you wanted to see me?" I asked, walking into his office. He was about sixty-five years old, with gray hair and jowls that reminded me of that cartoon dog.

"Yes, Tom," he said somewhat pleasantly. "How's your mother?"

"She's okay," I answered, unsure of where he was going. "She's determined to stay at the house, though. I call her every night, just to check on her," I said, though I got the feeling he didn't really care. He was simply making polite conversation until he got to the subject he was after.

"I saw that young intern of yours at the funeral..."

And there it was.

"His name is Cooper."

"Yes, that's it," he said, like he didn't know. "Cooper Jones." He stared at me for a long moment. "You seemed very... familiar."

I couldn't believe it. I could not fucking believe it. "He's my boyfriend, if that's the information you're fishing for," I said, not caring if he didn't like my tone. "Actually, we now live together."

Robert tilted his head. "Were you seeing him while he was your intern?"

Fuck.

"No," I lied. "Strictly professional while he was here."

"I'm glad to hear that," Robert said with a smug smile. "Because you know it's a breach of company policy to date staff. Particularly impressionable interns."

I almost laughed at that. Cooper was anything but impressionable, but that was not Robert's point. I'd broken company protocol, and we both knew it.

"Am I being officially reprimanded?" I asked him outright.

He smiled a little more genuinely this time. "Heavens, no," he said, though I didn't believe him. "Though I am curious about one thing."

"What's that?"

"Why didn't you recommend we hire him?"

There were two ways I could answer that question. I could tell him I hadn't wanted him to work here because then we couldn't date and basically admit that I'd been seeing him while he'd worked here. Or I could lie and tell him I didn't think Cooper was good enough.

Instead, I answered his question with a question. A conversational trait I *knew* Robert detested. Maybe that was why I did it. Sure, Robert had mentored me when I started at Brackett and Golding, and I admired him professionally. But as employees in this company, we were on an equal footing, so the words *fuck you* echoed in my mind.

Cooper was starting to wear off on me.

"Why are you bringing this up now?" I asked. "One month after my father's funeral, where you saw Cooper and me together. Why now? Why not the day I came back to work?" Then it dawned on me. It had taken a month for him to find out information. "Did it honestly take you that long to find out anything on him? Because really, Robert, you just could have asked me."

"A little defensive, don't you think, Tom?" he asked dismissively.

"Not at all," I said. "But tell me this, Robert. You've known I am gay for five years. Why act all homophobic and discriminatory now?"

That stopped him. Two very carefully chosen words, with a lawsuit ring to them. Not that I would go down that route, but he didn't know that.

"Tom, that's not what this is about," he replied. "That's not why I wanted to speak to you at all."

He had made me so damn angry I wanted to let him have a piece of my mind. I'd probably already said too much, but I needed to play his game. "I'm glad to hear that, Robert," I said. "Because we wouldn't want to have a conversation one might deem inappropriate."

"No, we wouldn't," he replied with a knowing smile.

"Robert, if you're alluding to an official reprimand, please, by all means, have it on my desk by lunchtime and I'll have my lawyer look it over. But just so you know, I first met Cooper through my son, Ryan. Not Brackett and Golding. I chose him to be my intern because he was the most talented one there." Then I added, "But you're right about one thing. I didn't want him to work here. I called Louisa Arlington and lined up an interview for him, but he got the job on his own merit. And she has since thanked me for suggesting he work with her."

I stood up and went to the door. "And if you want to know the reason why I didn't want him to work here, it wasn't because I wanted to be with him and couldn't because of *company policy*." I took a breath to make sure my voice was steady when I spoke. "I didn't want him to work here because the staunch traditionalism and lack of free thinking would have suffocated him."

And with that, I walked out.

I stormed back to my office, past Jennifer, who had the grace to leave me alone long enough to calm down.

I waited for an official letter to come from the Chairman of the Board, upon recommendation from Robert. But it never came.

By the time I got home, I was calmer and had let most of the residual anger go. I knew Cooper had wanted me to cook, but I really wasn't in the mood. I had dinner ordered by the time he got home. "I ordered you the Thai fish you wanted," I told him.

He finished putting his messenger bag on the table and pulled his tie off, then he gave me a proper kiss. "If I hadn't come home right now, would you have pretended you cooked it thinking I'd be all impressed and love-struck?" he asked, batting his eyelashes.

I snorted. "There's no way I could fake that kind of cooking skill."

"You cook just fine," he said, opening the fridge and pulling out two bottled waters and handing me one. "I went to see your doctor today," he said casually. "I called to make an appointment, he had a vacancy, so I went. Had all the usual screening tests done." Then he sighed dramatically. "No prostate exam, though."

I laughed. "Did you ask for one?"

He pretended to be offended. "Not on the first date! I'm not that kind of guy."

Still smiling, I took a sip of water. "What else did he say?"

"That you were handsome and dreamy."

"He did not," I said flatly. "He's a straight man."

"Oh," Cooper said with a grin. "Maybe that was me who said that."

"You're such a dork."

"Dork?" he replied. "Really, Tom? No one's used the word 'dork' since the nineties."

"Oh my God," I cried sarcastically. "They should archive it with Olde English. The nineties were sooooo long ago."

Cooper rolled his eyes at me. "So how was your day, anyway?"

"Well," I said slowly, "I had a very interesting conversation with Robert Chandler this morning."

"The old fogey with the gray-helmet hair?"

I snorted again. "Yes, that's him."

"What did you talk about?"

"You."

"Me?"

I nodded, then relayed the entire conversation to him.

"An official reprimand, Tom!" he cried. "Jesus Christ!"

"I never got one," I said, trying to calm him down. "I think he was just trying to gauge my reaction, that's all. So in hindsight, I probably shouldn't have lost my temper."

"That wasn't losing your temper," Cooper said, shaking his head. "Telling him to mind his own fucking business would be losing your temper."

I smiled. "Actually, I thought of you and almost told him to fuck off."

"I would have," Cooper replied. "What we do is none of his fucking business."

"Well, technically it was when you were my intern," I amended. "I knew I was breaking company policy by seeing you." Then I shrugged. "And I did it anyway."

"Ugh," he groaned. "That's so not fair."

Then dinner arrived, and he spent the entire meal stabbing his fish with his fork or pointing it at me while he ranted about the fucking politics of fascist corporate leaders who should have retired in the Middle Ages.

All I could do was smile at him.

"Why doesn't it bother you?" he asked.

"It did when it first happened this morning," I said. "I was livid. But at the end of the day, it's just one reprimand. We don't work together anymore. I'm not bringing any disrepute onto the Brackett and Golding reputation with a sexual harassment case or anything. He's got nothing else on me."

"Yeah," Cooper agreed. "But what's he really after?"

"What do you mean?"

"You've been friends with this guy for years," he answered. "He went to your father's funeral, and now this? It doesn't seem right."

"Maybe he's not as tolerant of same-sex couples as he thought he was," I answered.

Cooper growled. "Well, maybe someone should suggest the old fart retires and let the rest of the twenty-first century get on with their work."

I picked up his plate and gave him a kiss. "I love the way you think."

"What if you get to work tomorrow and there's a letter on your desk?"

"Then I'll deal with that tomorrow." I walked into the kitchen and he followed me, leaned against the counter and crossed his arms. "But let's not worry about it anymore tonight. What's done is done." He didn't seem exactly happy with the idea, but with a pout and a sigh, he let it go.

Later that night when I was getting ready for bed, a naked Cooper snuggled down on my side of the mattress. "The doctor said something else," he said quietly.

I threw our dirty underwear into the hamper. "What's that?"

"He said he'd spoken to you about the possibility of unprotected sex."

Oh.

Cooper smiled. "It's okay, Tom. He never told me what you said or anything. Just that it's something we should talk about, if it's something we might want to do."

"I, um..." I climbed onto the bed and took his hand. "I didn't mention it to you yesterday, because I don't know how I feel about it."

Cooper nodded thoughtfully. "It's weird, huh? Condoms are just something I assumed I'd always need." He shrugged one shoulder. "It's not just a safety thing, but it's a security thing. I'm not sure if I'm explaining that correctly."

I snuggled in beside him and kissed him softly. "I understand exactly what you mean. And when he first mentioned it to me, I was like no way, it's condoms or nothing." Then I exhaled slowly. "But the more I thought about it..."

Cooper leaned up on his arm so he could look at me. "The more you thought about it, what?"

"Well, I'm not opposed to sharing that experience with you," I hedged. "As long as we're both given the all-clear and we both want it."

He bit his lip. "I'm not sure."

"Truthfully, neither am I. But we have a few weeks before you get your test results, and even then we don't have to agree to it. We can wait a year or ten years before we need to decide."

Cooper smiled and settled down into the crook of my arm. "Thank you for understanding."

I kissed the top of his head. "Thank you for understanding, too."

He sighed contentedly, and after a long moment, he asked, "What do you think Robert will say to you at work tomorrow?"

I tightened my hold on him. "I don't know. It doesn't matter. If he wants to reprimand me for dating you, then let him. I don't care." I rolled over so I faced him, so our noses were almost touching. "Because given the chance to go back and do it again, I wouldn't change a thing. I should be sorry for breaking company policy, but I'm not. I'm not sorry at all, and if he has a problem with that, he can get fucked."

Cooper laughed and put his hand to my face. "I think I'm starting to rub off on you."

I kissed him with smiling lips. "I know you are," I agreed. "But if I'm going to get reprimanded over anything, it'll be because I told him the reason I didn't want you to work with me was because people like him would suffocate someone like you with their institutionalized way of thinking."

Cooper's eyes drilled into mine. "But you don't think like that."

"Not anymore," I whispered.

He smiled, slow and shy. "I think that's the best compliment you've ever given me." I opened my mouth to speak, but he put his thumb over my lips. "Shh, don't ruin it."

I took his thumb between my lips, sucking it into my mouth. His eyes darkened and he groaned low in his throat.

I pulled back, giving him a smirk. "Want to put something else in my mouth?"

He nodded. "God, yes."

"Get up on your knees," I urged him. So while I lay on the bed, he knelt near my face, offering me his dick.

I slid one arm around his thigh and ran my fingers over his ass to cup his balls from behind while I took his cock into my mouth. He gripped the headboard and moaned, threading his fingers through my hair.

"Oh fuck, Tom," he gasped, then moaned long and slow.

I worked him over while his thighs trembled and his cock grew impossibly harder. He was trying not to thrust into my mouth, trying to restrain himself, so I sucked him harder, deeper. He stuttered out a warning, "Tom, gonna—gonna—fuck, Tom, I'm gonna come."

So with a final thrust, I took him into my throat and his whole body shook as he cried out some strangled cry and he came.

When he could form coherent words, he said, "Your turn."

I stopped him. "No, just for you tonight."

He was too spent to argue. He burrowed himself into my side and fell asleep with a smile.

"GOOD MORNING, LIONEL," Cooper said cheerfully as we walked through the lobby.

"Good morning, Mr. Jones, Mr. Elkin," Lionel said, addressing us both with a smile.

"How's the weather out there today?" Cooper asked, looking out at the rather gray-looking New York day.

"Getting colder," Lionel said with a nod. "It'll be snowing before you know it."

"I trust Mrs. Lionel is well?" Cooper asked with a smile.

"She's still wonderful," the old man said proudly. "Don't know what I ever did to get so lucky."

"Aw," Cooper said. "Tom says the same thing about me!"

I rolled my eyes, and Lionel tried not to smile. Instead, he said, "You gentlemen have a great day."

"Thank you, Lionel," I said. "Same to you."

Cooper and I stepped out onto the sidewalk, ready to go our separate ways. "Don't let that Robert dickhead say anything to you today," Cooper said. "I'd hate to have to come over and kick some old guy's ass."

I couldn't help but laugh. "Do you have some tough-guy persona I haven't seen yet?"

"Absolutely," he said brightly. "I have a black belt in sarcasm, and my wit is like lightning."

I laughed. "Goodbye, Cooper."

I walked to work with a smile. Although I was dreading another *meeting* with Robert, he never spoke to me, came near me or even looked at me. That was more than fine by me.

Jennifer was her cool, professional self, but she looked troubled by my conversation with Robert, or at least by the residual tension that seemed to settle over the office because of it.

Never one to look like anything affected her, she seemed a little on edge all week. When she brought in some files on Friday, I asked her if she was okay. "Yes, I'm fine," she said plainly. "Why wouldn't I be?"

"Just with my meeting with Robert earlier this week, I don't want you to worry about it, that's all," I told her.

"Nonsense," she said, dismissing the notion completely.

Of course she said she was fine. On the outside, nothing seemed to faze her. I remembered when I'd told her I'd separated from Sofia because I was gay, she hadn't even blinked. She'd just asked if I was okay, then proceeded to hand me my coffee and tell me about my day's appointments.

But this seemed to have put a chink in her well-polished armor. Knowing Jennifer, if she didn't want to discuss it, it wasn't up for conversation, so I let it go.

I went about my work and was having a rather productive afternoon, when my phone buzzed. Cooper's name flashed across the screen, and I smiled as I answered. Without so much as a hello, and not giving me time to speak, he said, "Oh my God, Tom. I got it." His speech was fast and excited.

I couldn't help but smile. "Got what?"

"The job!" he cried. "I got the Xavier Baurhenn contract."

"Oh, Cooper, that's excellent," I said. I was grinning, knowing what this meant to him.

"He saw my proposal and loved it."

"Of course he did," I said. "Because it was amazing."

I could tell he was grinning when he spoke. "He said it was a standout."

"I thought you weren't showing him until Monday?"

"We weren't supposed to," he explained. "But Xavier called and asked Louisa how we were coming along with the prelims, and she told him I'd done more than just the prelims. She told him I was almost done, so he came over to look at it."

"And?"

"And he freakin' loved it," he cried, and I laughed.

"We're going out for celebratory drinks," Cooper said. "You have to come, Tom. It's my first contract and you need to be there."

"Of course I'll be there."

An hour later, still dressed in my work suit, I walked into the young and trendy bar, through the young and trendy crowd, to find some young, trendy, good-looking guy with his arm around Cooper.

CHAPTER THREE

COOPER'S FACE lit up when he saw me, as though he couldn't get away from the other guy quick enough. He left him standing there, and the others he was talking to, and quickly walked over to me. He kissed me, right on the mouth.

"Thank God you're here," he said.

"Everything okay?" I asked.

"Yep," he said brightly. Then he took my hand and led me back toward the group of people he was with. "I want you to meet everyone."

I was introduced to a Skye, Tyson, Ben—all of whom gave me wide-eyed nods—then Cooper turned and proudly, nervously, introduced me to Xavier, the guy who had had his arm around him.

"Hello," I said, shaking his hand. He was about twenty years younger than I'd expected him to be. "It's a pleasure to meet you."

Xavier shook my hand firmly, then looked at Cooper. "You said his name was Tom!"

Cooper smiled. "It is."

Xavier shook his head. "Not Thomas fucking Elkin."

Cooper burst out laughing. "He's just Tom to me."

I smiled at Xavier. "It's true. I am just Tom to him."

Cooper slid his arm around my waist and leaned into me. "Can I get you a drink?" he asked me.

"Shouldn't I be buying?" I asked. "I believe congratulations are in order."

Cooper rolled his eyes and ignored me. "Scotch and soda?"

I gave him a nod and was left with Cooper's colleagues and Xavier staring at me.

One of the young guys, Ben, stuck his hand out. "Mr. Elkin, it's a real pleasure. I've admired your work for years."

Skye was next. She shook my hand nervously. "I had no idea when Cooper talked of Tom that he meant you," she said.

Before I could be any more embarrassed, Louisa Arlington, Cooper's boss, saw me and made her way over. She kissed my cheek. "Tom, it's so good to see you!"

"Louisa, you look great," I told her honestly. She did. She'd lost weight or gotten taller or done something to her hair.

She smiled genuinely. "Cooper's been doing some excellent work," she went on to say. "He has an eye for fine detail."

"He puts the hours in," I told her.

"Cooper told me about your father," she said with a kind smile. "I'm very sorry."

"Thanks. And I'm sorry Cooper had to leave Philly early," I said. "He worked hard on that project."

"And it showed," she said with a nod. "It was his work on that project that got him seen by Xavier, here," she said, including him in our conversation.

Cooper came back with two drinks and handed me one. He smiled and again slid his arm around my waist.

He wasn't being possessive. He was just showing Xavier, who quite possibly wanted him, that he was with me. Well, maybe just a little possessive.

And while we talked and mingled with his coworkers and with Xavier, it wasn't lost on me that he'd not told any of them about me. Well, he'd told them about a 'Tom' but not who I was exactly. I was a little put out at first, thinking maybe he didn't want them to know he was dating a man twice his age. But then it occurred to me that it was me who had insisted he work for Arlington so people wouldn't mistake his talent for my reputation.

So as much as I didn't really like it, I had no right to complain.

For most of the night, Cooper was with me. He either had his arm around my waist or his hand on my back, my ass, or my arm. But when Cooper got chatting with Ben, Skye and Tyson, it left me alone with Xavier.

"He's very talented," Xavier said. He was looking over at Cooper, smiling as he sipped his drink. "I've worked with him a lot over these last few weeks, and he has a gift."

"He does."

"I just think it's funny that in all that time, talking about architecture the way he does, he never mentioned you."

"He's professional," I agreed lightly.

Xavier nodded thoughtfully. "I wouldn't have pictured him to like older men," he said casually. "Just with how vibrant he is, he has so much energy. Thought he'd be with someone his own age, that's all."

The little fucking punk was giving me attitude! Implying he knew Cooper better than me and that Cooper would be better off with someone his own age. So I smiled at him. "Maybe he should be, maybe not. I'm sure there's a lot you don't know about him. One thing I will say, though, with all due respect"—which was minimal—"is that what Cooper does outside of your project isn't really your concern."

With that, I said, "Excuse me. It was nice meeting you," and I left him there, and walked over to where Cooper was. I very deliberately slid my hand over his ass so Xavier could see it and offered to buy the next round of drinks.

By the time I got back from the bar, Xavier was in my place. There was no doubt—he wanted Cooper. He was also a pompous little brat. When the group had decided they were headed to a nightclub, Louisa put up her hands and gracefully declined their offer.

"You'll come out with us, won't you, Cooper?" Xavier asked loudly, so everyone could hear. "You're not ready to call it a night yet, are you?"

Cooper's eyes darted to mine, and I shrugged. "You can go," I said.

His eyes narrowed briefly at me, then he turned to Xavier. "No, I won't. Thanks for the offer, but I have an early start tomorrow. I have your project details to finalize."

"But it's the weekend!" Xavier said as though it was a foreign concept, and I wondered whether he'd ever worked a weekend in his life.

"No rest for the wicked," Cooper said with a smile, though it was hardly genuine. He glanced at me again, and it took me a second to recognize the look on his face. I'd never seen it before. Well, I'd seen it, but it was never directed at me.

Cooper was pissed off at me.

He announced that he should be going, did the rounds of smiling goodbyes, shook hands with Xavier, and told him he'd see him Monday, and without our usual conversation, we went home.

By the time we walked through the door and I'd pulled off my tie and shoes, Cooper was quiet, his anger was just bubbling under the surface. I had no idea what he was angry about, what I'd done wrong, but I knew with Cooper it would only be a matter of time before he told me.

I asked him if he wanted coffee as I set the machine and got two cups from the cupboard. His silence was unnerving. Cooper was never silent. So I figured I'd throw it out there. "Xavier is impressed by you. Though I didn't realize he was gay."

"Does that matter?" Cooper asked.

"Well, no," I replied. "Of course not." Then I shrugged.

"Then why bring it up?"

"Just that you never mentioned it."

"Because it's not important," he said curtly. "You should know that, Tom."

"I do know that, Cooper," I said calmly. "But he basically told me he thought you should be with someone like him, not me."

"He said that?"

"Not exactly," I conceded. "But he alluded to it."

"What did you say?"

"Nothing. Just smiled at him, told him maybe you should. But that it was none of his business, and that's when I walked over to you."

"You said *maybe I was better off with someone like him?*" he asked like he couldn't believe it.

"I did tell him, very diplomatically, that who you're with doesn't affect how you do your job. But apart from that, what was I *supposed* to say?" I asked. "I'm just not sure how I feel about people like that."

"Feel about what?" Cooper asked incredulously. "What is there to *feel* about it?"

"I don't know... jealousy. Insecurity. Self-doubt."

Cooper's mouth fell open. "Who? *You?*"

"Yes, me!" I replied. "He'd be perfect for you! He's brilliant, successful... younger."

Cooper groaned. "I don't want him! I've never even thought of him like that! He's an immature little brat whose daddy has handed him everything. And stop with the 'I'm too old for you' bullshit, okay? Because I'm sick of fucking hearing about it."

His outburst surprised me. "Okay," I said.

"Jesus, Tom," he went on to say, "your whole 'I'll set you free if it's what you want' mindset drives me insane! It's so *noble* of you," he added sarcastically.

I'd obviously touched a nerve. "Well, it's true. I love you enough to not stand in your way."

Cooper rolled his eyes and groaned loudly again. "That right there! Some people might find that sweet, Tom, but you know what? It pisses me off!"

"Jesus Christ, Cooper," I said back to him. "I will never win with you! What the hell am I supposed to do?"

"I want you to get all pissy," he shot back at me. "I want you to show some asshole who might hit on me that I fucking belong to you, that's what. When the likes of *Xavier* tell you they think I should be with them instead, I want you to tell them to back the fuck off. I want you to tell them I am yours. Tell them you're the one I go home with, you're the one I want." He ran his hand through his hair. "I want you to show some emotion. I don't want you to act like if I *did* leave with someone else that you wouldn't give a shit. It's not that hard, Tom."

"Wouldn't give a shit?" I asked. "It would kill me,

Cooper. Do you think by my wanting the best for you, if that means you moving on, that it wouldn't fucking kill me? Jesus, Cooper, you're *it* for me. I want everything with you. I want to spend the rest of my life with you—I'd fucking marry you, Cooper, in a fucking heartbeat. I want you to have it all, so how could I ever stand in your way?"

Cooper's mouth fell open and he slowly raised his hands so he could rub his forehead. "For the love of fucking God, Tom, please don't tell me that was a proposal. Because fuck, that was the most woeful excuse for a marriage proposal ever."

I exhaled in a rush. The argument in me was gone. "No, it wasn't. But I would marry you. And I do know you love me; that's not what I'm insecure about," I said. "I just want you to have everything. I don't want you to choose anyone else, and it scares the shit out of me that one day you will." I ran my hands through my hair. "To be honest, Cooper, I'm not even sure I know what we're arguing about."

Cooper sighed and walked over to me. He fisted my shirt at my stomach. "We're not arguing. It's just when someone basically tells you they want me, it'd be nice if you acted like you cared."

I cupped his face. "I care, so fucking much," I said before I kissed him. "Don't ever think I don't care. It's just the likes of Xavier don't deserve the reaction. He's your first contract client, and as much as I'd have liked to tell him to fuck off, I couldn't. I wouldn't do anything to jeopardize your work."

"Ugh," Cooper groaned and leaned his forehead on my collarbone.

This whole outburst was just so not Cooper. I rubbed his back. "Now would you like to tell me what's really bothering you?"

He lifted his face and his eyes flickered with doubt. It wasn't something I saw very often. He frowned. "I know he likes me, I'm not stupid."

"So?"

"So what if he only picked my proposal because he thought he could have me with it?"

"Oh, Cooper, sweetheart," I said softly, running my hand down his face. "He picked yours because it was the best."

Cooper huffed. "The guy doesn't even know his left from his right."

I smiled. "He's a Baurhenn. His family has been in the real estate development field for decades. So his parents or grandparents might hold the purse strings, and he might not know the technical terms, but he knows good architecture when he sees it."

"I just thought, when he was trying to get me to go out with him, that that's all he wanted me for," Cooper said quietly. "That it wasn't my work. I put hours into that project."

I shook my head. "Have you got a copy of your project blueprints here?"

"On my laptop," he said with a nod. "Why?"

"Can you open it for me?" I asked. "I want to show you something. Just give me a sec."

I walked back out to the living room with a rolled set of blueprints that had yellowed with age.

Cooper was waiting for the CAD program to load on his laptop, and when his familiar plans came up on screen, he pushed his laptop out for me to look. That was when he noticed the old plans in my hand. "What are those?"

"These are the blueprints to my first ever contracted

job," I said, then I pointed to the laptop screen, "just like yours."

His eyes widened. "Really?"

"Yes."

"Can I look at them?"

"Please do," I said, unrolling the delicate paper. "I want you to look at them. Actually, I want you to tell me what you see."

Cooper almost frowned, and as I laid the plans flat on the table, I used the corner of his laptop as a paperweight and held the other side with my hand. Cooper stood right up close to me and put his hand on my hip as he scanned over the old plans.

"These are incredible."

"Well, no," I added. "Not compared to what I've done since, but these were my first project plans. Simple, residential, but mine."

Cooper traced his finger over the lines on the paper down to the bottom right-hand corner. He read the words out loud, almost reverently. "Drawn by Thomas Elkin. July 13th, 1991." He looked at me and sighed. "That was the year I was born."

"Yeah, thanks," I said, rolling my eyes. "Don't rub it in."

"No," he said quickly. "I mean, I think that's significant, don't you?"

Oh.

"Oh, um..." I paused. "I hadn't thought of it like that." I smiled at the sentiment. "I actually wanted you to look at both of these plans, my very first and yours, and tell me what you see."

There were huge differences between the two. Not that one was computer-generated on a laptop screen, and the other was a twenty-two-year-old, hand-drawn lithograph plan. The difference was in the complexity, in the inventiveness. Cooper's plans were intricate, almost genius. And mine... were not.

Cooper saw it—he knew exactly what I meant. "Of course they're different. Technology from then to now is like night to day, Tom. Legal requirements, regulations, energy, it's all so *different*. So while the plans look a world apart, they're not really. Yours was a residential, mine's a commercial-residential."

He was trying to justify why his looked so new and grand, and mine looked pale in comparison. I chuckled at him and ran my hand up over his back. "Cooper, sweetheart, you want to know why yours is so much better than mine?"

He looked at me but said nothing, waiting for me to continue.

So I told him. "Because it *is* better than mine."

Cooper shook his head. "That's like comparing a computer from 1991 to a computer released today. You just can't."

"Look at them," I said to him again. "The fundamentals are the same, yes. But see this?" I asked, pointing to the laptop screen. "See how you've used this space? See how you've used the positive flow you've created through the commercial floor area and then the functionality of the apartments above it? How you've used the energy created by venting the window cavities to source the internal airflow..." I shook my head. "Cooper, I don't think you understand just how talented you are."

He stared at me and bit the inside of his lip. Then he shook his head.

"Cooper," I whispered. "You have more natural talent for this than I could have dreamed of at your age."

Still biting his lip, he had disbelief in his eyes. "Really?"

I gave him a smile and a kiss on the cheek. "Yes, really. So don't let clients like Xavier bother you too much. There will always be clients who grate on you."

"I have to work with him pretty closely on this for the next few months."

"So you be your professional self, and if he's still inappropriate toward you, go over his head. Ask Laura to speak to his supervisor, or his father, or whoever." Then I smiled. "And failing all of that, tell him young and successful isn't your thing. Tell him you like graying hair and a sagging ass."

Cooper smiled and even managed a bit of a laugh, and he ran his hand over the curve of my ass and gave it a squeeze. "Graying hair, yes. Sagging ass, no."

Then he looked back over my paper blueprints and sighed. "I love these plans. I can't believe you don't have them framed or something."

I shrugged. "They've been up on the shelf in Ryan's closet. Who knows?" I said. "Maybe one day I will."

Cooper looked into my eyes and shook his head as though he couldn't believe something. "How do you do it?"

"Do what?"

"Know exactly what to say," he said. "Like showing me these." He waved his hand at the plans on the table. "Knowing it was exactly what I needed to hear." He smiled and sighed contentedly. He even leaned against me as he kept his gaze on the plans, but then he shook his head slowly. "And then you can completely screw something up as important as a move-in-with-me speech or a marry-me speech."

I could have argued the whole point, that it technically wasn't a proposal, but with Cooper, there was no point in arguing. In fact, I was just happy he hadn't freaked out when I'd even mentioned getting married. So instead of arguing, I playfully growled and pretended to bite his neck.

"Come on," he said, taking my hand and pulling me down the hallway.

"What about the plans?"

"Leave them," he said. "You might not be able to show that dickhead Xavier that I belong to you, but you can damn well show me."

MONDAY MORNING at work was interesting, to say the least. We had our usual senior staff meeting, and all the usual things were discussed—portfolios, budgets, projections, and schedules.

Robert never looked at me or even spoke to me, until we were walking out of the conference room.

"Nice photo in yesterday's paper," he said coolly.

I, of course, had no clue what he was talking about, but I replied with a cheery, "Thanks." And as soon as I was in my office, I googled *New York Times* and there on page six of the social pages was me, Cooper, and of all people, Xavier Baurhenn leaving the bar we were at on Friday night. I hadn't even known Xavier had left the same time as us.

But it was the story with the photo that made me both smile and cringe.

Esteemed architect Thomas Elkin and his boyfriend, Cooper Jones, and development heir Xavier Baurhenn, was written underneath the photograph. But the story itself read, *Thomas Elkin looks like the responsible dad driving the kids home after a night out, but he is, in fact, the live-in boyfriend of the much younger up-and-coming architect Cooper Jones.*

The article about us stopped at that and went on to talk about who else was seen out and about.

I picked up my phone and dialed Cooper's number. He answered the call with, "Look, I've already told you, I like my men with gray hair and a saggy ass."

I snorted into the phone. "Just as well."

"I only left you a mere two hours ago," he said brightly. "I know I'm amazing, but surely you don't miss me that much."

I sighed into the phone. He really was incorrigible. "Have you seen page eighty-seven of yesterday's *New York Times?* Well, page six of the social pages."

"No," he replied. "We didn't leave the apartment yesterday. Actually, we barely left the bedroom, remember?"

"Did you want to look it up online?" I asked a little impatiently.

"I already am," he answered, just as impatiently. "Holy shit!" He'd just seen the picture, obviously.

"That's what I thought."

"I didn't even see anyone with a camera when we left," he said.

"Neither did I. What the freakin' hell are we doing in the social pages?"

"Well, I'm awesome, and you're hot," he replied casually. "What's not to love? Well, at any rate, I think it's fantastic. The old and the new in New York."

"I'm being serious!" I cried. "It's ludicrous."

Then Cooper burst out laughing. "*You look like the responsible dad driving the kids home...* Oh my fucking God, it actually says that!"

"Yeah," I grumbled, "but you don't need to laugh about it."

And yet he was still laughing. The little shit.

"It's not that funny."

"I'm gonna send this to Mom and Dad," he said, still chuckling. "They might put it on the fridge."

"I don't think they're ready for that," I said.

"It's not like we're snogging in the gutter or anything," he replied. "You're not even holding my hand... Hey, you're not even holding my hand!"

I rolled my eyes, even though he couldn't see it. "You were pissed at me, remember? Because I didn't beat my chest and drag you back to my cave by your hair."

Cooper laughed into the phone, then he spoke like a caveman, "Cooper laugh. Tom. Make funny."

I couldn't help but laugh at that. "I'll see you at home tonight."

"Yes, and thanks for offering to cook Thai fish for dinner. Sounds great."

"I didn't," I started to say, but was only talking to a dial tone. I hung up the phone and rubbed my temples. I really should take a vitamin pill, a shot of Scotch, and one shot of adrenaline before having phone conversations with him.

CHAPTER FOUR

I WAS IN THE KITCHEN, trying to separate fillets of fish with one hand while I held my cell to my ear with the other. "Well, I'm trying to cook dinner," I mumbled into the phone. The line was quiet for a long moment. "Sofia?" I asked. "You still there?"

"Yes," she said. "What exactly are you cooking?"

"It's supposed to be some Thai fish thing."

She snorted out a laugh. "Seriously?"

"Cooper's mentioned it a few times," I told her. "I thought I'd try. We order it, so I know what it's *supposed* to taste like..."

She chuckled, somewhat amused at the idea. "Anyway, what I was calling for," she said lightly, "was that there are a few things up at the Casa that belonged to your dad. I thought you might want them."

"Oh."

"Yes, I know they came with the house, and technically they're mine," she said. "But they're not, Tom. They're yours. It's the old telescope in the study, and there's a chessboard in the den."

This was the Sofia I knew—this was the Sofia I'd been married to for twenty years. "Um, thank you, Sofia," I said. "That means a lot to me."

"It's no problem," she replied. "Not this weekend, but the weekend after, you're more than welcome to go up to get them. You and Cooper can stay... if you want."

I could hardly believe it. I smiled into the phone. "Thank you, Sofia." I wasn't thanking her for the offer of the Casa for a weekend. I was thanking her for her acceptance. "That means... that means a lot."

"It's okay, Tom," she said.

"So, what are your plans this weekend?" I asked. "You mentioned plans?"

Sofia cleared her throat. "Well, there might be someone..."

"Really?" I asked with a smile.

"Yes, Tom." Then she mumbled something about how the girls had set her up through a friend of a friend, how she'd seen him a few times since and his name was Phil. She seemed nervous but happy. It sounded like she was finally starting to move on.

"That's good, Sof," I said softly. "I'm so glad to hear it."

There was the familiar jingle of keys at the front door, and when the door opened, Cooper walked in. Well, it was more *New York Times* than Cooper. It was his legs and hips, but he was holding up the social page, page eighty-seven, with the picture of us on it.

I laughed at him, and he shook the paper and hollered, "We're in the *New York Times*, baby!"

"Is that Cooper?" Sofia asked, obviously hearing him through the phone.

"Yes, that's Cooper," I answered into the phone, making

Cooper lower the newspaper to see who I was talking to. "He's being... Cooper."

I grinned at him, walking around the kitchen island to kiss him. He swatted me with the newspaper and gave me a pouty smile. "That's for calling me names."

I chuckled, still holding the phone to my ear. "Thanks again, Sofia. I'll check with him and let you know, if that's okay?"

Realizing I was talking to my ex-wife, Cooper raised an eyebrow and walked into the kitchen. He inspected the fish and the tube of Thai spices and looked at me, rather alarmed. Then he called out, "Sofia, dear God, help me, he's going to try to cook!"

"Ignore him," I told her, knowing she'd heard him. I followed him into the kitchen. "I cook sometimes."

Cooper held out his hand, and reluctantly, I handed the phone over. While I separated the fish and dabbed it with a paper towel, Cooper spoke to Sofia. He gave her a commentary on my culinary skills and I heard her laugh through the phone. The entire conversation lasted all of thirty seconds. And when he slid my phone onto the counter, he sighed. "She loves me."

I rolled my eyes. "Well, she can take a number."

"She told me to tell you that you should cook more often."

"Of course she did."

"Even though you're cooking fish, when I specifically asked for chicken."

"You did not!"

"Well, I meant to," he said. "And she said you should stop looking so damn sexy in jeans with no socks and shoes," he said, looking at my feet.

I smiled at him. "Right. She said that."

Cooper nodded shamelessly. "She also said you were lucky to have someone as awesome as me."

"Oh, yes, we all know that," I said flatly.

"Then she said you should stop what you're doing, drop to your knees in the kitchen and give me a blow job."

I laughed at him. "Are you sure she said that?" I asked. "It wasn't a very long conversation, and that's hardly an icebreaker for short conversations with ex-wives."

"Yes, that's what she said," Cooper said seriously. "Or something like that. I was having trouble concentrating. I was distracted by your naked feet."

I washed my hands in the sink, dried them on the dishtowel, then walked over to stand in front of him. I pulled his chin between my thumb and forefinger and pressed his lips to mine. Sliding my hand down his neck, his chest, further down his stomach and even lower, I expertly popped the button on his suit pants with one hand.

He smiled against my lips then he nodded. "Do it."

I slowly lowered to my knees and, right there in the kitchen, undid his suit pants and freed his semi-hard dick from his briefs. I took him into my mouth and sucked his cock to life.

I listened to him moan, and just before my eyes closed, lost to the feeling of him in my mouth, I saw his fingers grip the marble countertop. I loved how his cock hardened, how it felt like silk on steel in my mouth—hot, hard, and pulsing.

I wrapped my arms around his thighs and opened my throat to take all of him. I skimmed my fingers between the cheeks of his ass, over his hole to his balls, and with a strangled cry, he came. His cock swelled and lurched in my mouth as he tried not to thrust into me, and his come shot thickly down my throat.

I licked him clean, and when I let go of his hips, he

slumped against the countertop and slid down so he sat on the floor in front of me. He had a blissful, lazy smile and his eyes were heavy-lidded. He chuckled. "Jesus, Tom."

"You're gonna have to get up," I told him.

He took a second to focus on me, then he grinned. "Why?"

"Because I'm old and my knees are locked up from kneeling on the floor."

He laughed, really loudly. I pushed his shoulder. "It's not that funny, asshole. Now help me get up."

He was still laughing but got to his feet and pulled me up. He slowly tucked his spent cock back into his briefs, making sure I watched, then took my face in his hands and kissed me. He was still smiling.

"I suppose I should cook dinner now," he said. "Considering you just ate."

"You're such a little shit," I said. Then I squeezed his ass and gently pushed him out of the kitchen. "You go get changed, I'm cooking."

"Only if I get dessert later on," he said as he walked toward the hall. "But I'll make sure your knees don't lock up."

I was frying fish and still pouting by the time he came back out. He'd changed into cargos and an old college shirt, looking like he was about to play football in the park. I huffed at him. "If you don't mind not looking so fucking cute when I'm mad at you, thanks."

He slid his arms around me from behind and nuzzled my neck. I could tell he was smiling. "Don't be mad," he mumbled into the skin behind my ear. "You're perfect and gorgeous, so incredibly sexy, even if your old knees find tiles unforgiving."

I sighed. "You know, maybe I wouldn't have such a

complex about my age around you if you'd stop making fun of it."

Cooper stood back, and with a hand on my shoulder, he turned me around. There was no joking in his eyes, only concern and a seriousness I rarely saw in him. He opened his mouth, unsure of how to say something. Then he shook his head and whispered, "I don't mean it. I don't care about the age difference, I promise. I just joke about it... well, because that's what I do. I'm sorry. I'm sorry, I didn't—"

I put my hand to his lips and smiled at him. "I know you don't mean anything by it."

He shook his head, and he looked genuinely worried. "I don't. I don't mean anything by it. Don't be mad. I'm fucking cute, remember?"

I pretended to have to think about it.

So then he kissed me.

All-consuming, hands, lips, mouth, and tongue. Soft, slow, deep and sure, he held my face to his and kissed me like I'd never been kissed.

I forgot about the sizzling fish. Hell, I forgot my own name.

He pulled away, licked his lips, and took the spatula out of my hand, while I stood there, dazed and out of breath.

Cooper turned the fish in the pan and nodded smugly.

I exhaled in a rush and wiped my thumb across my bottom lip, feeling where he'd just been. "Jesus, Cooper. You can kiss."

"You're not the first person to tell me that."

"I better be the last."

Cooper turned the fish again. "Is that some Thomas Elkin way of telling me you want to be with me forever?"

I leaned against the countertop and sighed. "I'm

pleading the Fifth on that, because no matter what I say, it will be wrong."

Cooper laughed at that. "Yes, it probably will."

Seeing the fish was nearly done, I grabbed two plates. "It seems whenever I ask something, it's wrong."

"Only the big stuff."

I snorted. "Good to know."

Cooper plated the fish, threw on some sliced lemon, and I carried the salad and cutlery to the table. He sat at the table, still smiling. "What did Sofia call for?" he asked as he dished up the salad.

"There are a few things that belonged to my dad at the Casa," I said. "She offered for us to have the place to ourselves next weekend."

"The Casa?"

I nodded, spearing the first mouthful of fish. "Do you think you might want to spend the weekend in the Hamptons with a sexy, older man?"

"Do you know any?" he asked.

I tasted the fish. "Mmm, this is really good. And yes, I think I know someone who might be available."

Cooper slipped a forkful of fish into his mouth and smiled as he ate. "This is good," he said, finally swallowing his food. "So is this guy hung?"

"Like a horse," I answered. "Or so he's been told."

Cooper laughed, but we ate in silence until our plates were almost empty. "My next two weeks are busy as hell, so I'll probably look forward to a weekend away," he said, leaning back in his chair. "I'll be working with Xavier, so God knows I'll be needing some serious 'sexy older man who's hung like a horse' time."

I pushed my plate away, leaned back in my chair, and smiled. "Then you shall have it."

Cooper rubbed his stomach. "Dinner was good. I should cook more often."

"Cook?" I scoffed. "You turned the fish in the pan."

"Like a chef," he said proudly. "Oh," he said as though he'd just remembered, "I spoke to my mom today. I told her about the photo in the paper. I emailed it to her."

"What did she say?"

"That I'm awesome!" he said simply. "Well, she's my mom. Of course she thinks I'm awesome."

"I happen to think you're awesome too."

"You're my boyfriend. You have to say that."

"I call you a lot of things."

"I know. Some of them not very flattering, I might add."

"Such as?"

"You call me a little shit all the time."

"Because you are... some of the time."

"I think I prefer the term sassy."

I laughed at that. "So, if I call you sassy, it will be like a secret code instead of little shit?"

"Exactly!" he said. "Like if I stop saying 'because you're old,' I could say you were being 'funny.'"

"Funny?"

Cooper nodded brightly, apparently thinking this was a great idea. "Mm-hm. Funny is much nicer than old."

"What if you wanted to actually call me funny?"

Cooper cocked his head and looked off into space. "Well, it hasn't happened yet."

"You're such a—"

Cooper raised one eyebrow. "I'm what?"

"Sassy. You're a sassy little shit."

Cooper sighed, trying not to smile. "Well, it's true. You can't teach an old dog new tricks."

COOPER WAS RIGHT. For the next week, work kicked his ass. Early mornings, late nights, but he never lost that buzz for what he was doing. He'd get home late and show me the latest developments, excitedly demonstrating what he'd done that day.

On Friday night, Cooper got in around eleven, and as he sat on the edge of the bed, he took his shoes and socks off and sighed tiredly. He said Xavier was still all over him like a rash, but he had told Xavier, again and again, he wasn't interested. "If he stands too close, I talk about you," Cooper said. "If he even looks at me like he's about to say something not work related, I talk about you."

I put my book on the bedside table and smiled. "Don't let him bother you."

"Does it bother you?" he asked, stripping down to his briefs.

"No," I said quietly. "If it upset you, then that would upset me, but he can *want* you all he likes. Doesn't mean he'll *get* you." I pulled back the bedspread and Cooper climbed onto the bed.

He rested his head on my chest and snuggled into my side. "No, it doesn't."

We'd had a similar conversation to this that had ended in a fight, so I was wary as to how this would go. I kissed the top of his head. "I trust you, sweetheart."

This time he didn't argue. Instead, he whispered, "Thank you," then he just kissed my chest, held me tighter, and fell asleep in my arms.

He worked most of the weekend at his office, which was fine. I got work done from home, but it was eerily quiet. No music, nothing to trip over on the floor, no smell of food cooking in the apartment, no one swearing at the coffee machine.

It wasn't lost on me just how much he brought to my life.

Or how much I missed him when he wasn't there.

When he got home late on Sunday, I asked him if he wanted me to heat his dinner for him. He shook his head tiredly, and without a word, he took my hand and led me to bed.

He was tired, his movements were unhurried, his kisses slow and languid. "I really need you," he said gruffly. "Please, Tom." It didn't take much for me to be turned on by him.

I laid him on his stomach on the bed, and I lifted his ass. Slowly, tenderly, I readied him for me, and when I finally pushed my sheathed cock inside him, he arched his back and moaned.

I lay down over him, filling him completely. His eyes were closed and I slowly rocked my hips into him, savoring every moment. "Fuck," he moaned, long and low.

I kissed his neck, his shoulder, everywhere I could reach, while I thrust slowly into his ass. Cooper put his hands over mine, threading my fingers with his, and spread his thighs even wider.

I was buried so far inside him, every inch of me, and he lifted his ass for more. I rocked harder, I thrust deeper, and when his ass squeezed my cock, I couldn't hold off anymore. "Gonna come," I rasped in his ear.

He threw his head back and groaned while I filled the condom, deep inside him.

When I pulled out of him, I rolled him over. His eyes were closed, and he was smiling, his cock still hard. "You didn't come," I stated softly.

"Didn't need to," he replied sleepily, still with his eyes shut. "Just needed you."

I discarded the condom and licked the length of him, from his balls to the glistening tip of his cock. When I took him into my mouth, I slipped my finger into his still-slicked ass in search of his gland.

He bucked his hips, gripped the sheets and his eyes shot open. "Fuck!" he croaked out.

I sucked and licked and rubbed and swiped his prostate until he came with a hoarse cry. His body convulsed, wracked with waves of pleasure. Completely spent, bone-less and smiling, he fell asleep.

THE NEXT WEEK was much the same. He worked hard, as did I, and I missed him terribly. I still got a text message when he had a spare moment, a phone call at work every now and then, though he sounded tired.

He'd come home late every night, crawling into bed and falling asleep, only to wake up and go into work early. I knew he had to do it. Long hours came with a successful career. So as much as I missed him, I understood.

On Thursday night after work when I walked into the lobby of our apartment, Lionel beamed. "Special delivery for you, Mr. Elkin," he said, the crinkles at his eyes telling me it was a genuine smile.

I walked over to the reception desk, where there was a wrapped box and a bouquet of a dozen red roses. "Are these for me?"

Lionel nodded. "I think someone misses you."

My eyes darted to the doorman's. "Is there a card?"

"Of course," Lionel answered, handing me a small white envelope. "But Mr. Jones phoned ahead. He wanted to make sure it arrived. He said to say he'll be late again, and thank you for understanding."

I grinned so hard it was ridiculous, thanked Lionel, then took my gifts and went upstairs.

I opened the card first.

Saw this. It reminded me of you, of where it all began.

I ripped open the wrapping on the box, confused at first at what I saw. Then I burst out laughing and my heart warmed in my chest.

Of all the things it could have been, it was a box of fucking Lego.

Of where it all began...

The Architecture Lego of the Sydney Opera House.

Where we'd gone together, where we'd first made love, where I'd first realized the lines had blurred, where I'd been falling in love with him.

Where it all began.

CHAPTER FIVE

WHEN COOPER GOT HOME, it was almost midnight. I was sitting on the sofa with the coffee table in front of me, music playing softly. I'd drunk a bottle of wine and had almost finished the Sydney Opera House.

He set his messenger bag down at the door, looked at the empty bottle of wine, then at the Lego masterpiece, and finally he looked at me.

"Having fun?"

I chuckled at the look of disbelief on his face. "Actually, I am." Then I added, "But if you tell anyone, I'll deny it."

He fell onto the sofa beside me with a sigh and kissed me soundly.

"You're up late."

"Someone gave me Lego."

Cooper laughed. "And flowers, I hope." He looked around the apartment and found the vase full of roses on the middle of the dining table.

When he turned back to me, just about to speak, I slid my hand along his jaw, leaned in, and kissed him. "Thank you. No one has ever bought me flowers before."

His eyes widened. "No one?"

"No one, ever."

Cooper smiled proudly, but then his brow furrowed. "What about Lego? Has anyone ever bought you Lego?"

I couldn't help but chuckle at him. "I had wooden blocks as a kid. No Lego."

Cooper leaned back into the sofa and pulled his tie off. He was exhausted. "I saw it and thought of you," he said, smiling tiredly. "Going to Sydney was like the beginning of us, wasn't it?"

"It was," I agreed. I looked back at the almost-completed Lego Opera House. "What other Lego buildings did they have?"

Cooper had to think. "Um, Seattle Space Needle, Empire State Building, Eiffel Tower..."

"We should get them all," I suggested. "Then we can go see the real thing."

He raised one eyebrow at me. "The Eiffel Tower?"

"Absolutely," I said, squeezing his knee. "There is so much I'd love to show you in Paris... actually, there's a lot of Europe I'd love to show you."

Cooper leaned his head on the back of the sofa and smiled warmly at me. "I would love that."

"You're so tired," I stated the obvious. "Come on, let's get you into bed." I pulled him to his feet, and while I turned off lights, he walked down the hall, stripping off his shirt and vest as he went. He dropped them where he was. I picked them up as I followed him, then his crumpled suit pants off the bedroom floor.

He was crawling into bed, wearing only his briefs. "Are we leaving after work tomorrow to head up to the Hamptons?"

"Yeah, if you want."

He nodded. "Looking forward to it," he said with a yawn.

"How was Xavier?"

Cooper groaned. "I don't want to talk about him. He's a sleaze."

I got into bed and pulled up the covers. "Has he hit on you again?"

"All the time," Cooper mumbled, almost asleep. "But I'm not privileged. He's like that with everyone."

I leaned over and kissed his closed eyelid. "Go to sleep, sweetheart. Thank you again for my gifts."

"Welcome," he mumbled, and his lip curled up in a tired smile.

"I love you," I whispered.

"'Cause I'm awesome," came his mumbled response. His hand reached for mine, he threaded our fingers, and brought our hands to his chest. His breathing evened out, and he fell into sleep.

COOPER BROUGHT SO much work with us when we went up to the Casa, I wondered if it was even worth the break away.

It also reminded me of what Sofia had put up with for years. I'd worked so much when I was Cooper's age and for the twenty years after. I'd taken work with me when we vacationed, on weekends and nights out.

I didn't begrudge Cooper for the workload. I didn't envy him either. But it was something I understood.

I carried in the overnight bag of clothes and dropped it

at the foot of the stairs, while Cooper unloaded his messenger bag onto the dining table.

It was ten in the morning, but Cooper hadn't eaten before we'd left. He'd barely woken up. "Are you hungry?" I asked him. "If you want, I'll make you something to eat while you have a swim to wake yourself up?"

Cooper smiled. "You just like to see me wet."

"True."

"Will you join me?"

"Maybe later," I said. "I want you to relax first. You've been working so hard. Relax first, work later."

"You relax me," he said, smirking at me. "You, wet, in the pool, with me. *That* would relax me."

I rolled my eyes. "I'm sure it would."

But then his eyebrows pinched, and he said, "We didn't bring any food. We can't eat Sofia's food, that'd be rude."

"I organized a grocery delivery yesterday. Sofia was here when it arrived."

Cooper walked over and pecked my lips with his. "You think of everything."

I smiled, but then I admitted, "Well, Jennifer asked if I wanted to have food delivered. She knew we were coming up here for the weekend and thought it was a good idea. She organized it."

"Remind me to thank Jennifer," Cooper said with a smile.

"She likes you."

"Of course she does." Then he took a fistful of my shirt and led me to the back doors, toward the pool. "Come on, old man, you're coming with me to get wet."

I tried to protest. "I'm not wearing swimming trunks."

Cooper laughed, opened the door, and pulled me outside. "You won't need them."

———

AFTER WE WERE both wet and *relaxed*, we got dried and dressed and Cooper suggested a walk on the beach before an early lunch.

He seemed to be a little quiet, which I presumed was from being tired, so I never questioned it. I just held his hand as we walked and was more resolved to make sure he had a relaxing weekend away.

The afternoon got cool, and Cooper started to organize his workspace at one end of the dining table. Sofia had left the two items from my father on the table, so I told Cooper I'd put them in the car so he had more room.

Cooper ran his hand over the telescope. "It's beautiful, Tom."

"It is," I agreed. "It was nice of Sofia to give it back to me. I didn't think of taking it when we split. She got the house and everything in it, and by the time it all went through, I just wanted to move on, you know?"

Cooper nodded thoughtfully. "Where will you put it?"

"I don't know," I answered honestly. "Somewhere in the apartment, or I'll store it or give it to Ryan."

"Do you play chess?" he asked, eyeing the wooden board.

"Not for a long time."

"You'll have to teach me how to play one day."

"I'd love that," I said, a slow smile spread across my face. "Not this weekend, though. You have enough work to keep you busy."

I took the telescope and the chessboard and loaded them into the trunk of the car, and when I came back inside, Cooper was leaning against the door frame looking at me.

"You okay?" I asked.

He smiled warmly. "I am. Are you?"

"Of course." I leaned in and kissed him. We turned and as we walked through the foyer into the living room, I noticed Cooper was looking around. He didn't look his usual comfortable, confident self.

I stopped and faced him. "What's bothering you?" I asked outright. "I mean, about this place? Since we got here, you've been quiet. I thought you were just tired, but now I'm not sure."

Cooper shrugged and spoke to the floor. "I don't know... it's a bit silly, actually."

"What is it?"

"Just that you designed this house. This is yours. For Sofia."

I knew something had been bothering him. "And Ryan," I corrected. "And for me. This holiday house was for me too."

"But it's not anymore."

"No, and you know what?" I asked rhetorically. "I don't regret it. Sure, I loved this house. I loved the fact that I could design something for my family. But I'm happy Sofia has it. I'm happy she wanted to keep it and not sell it to some stranger. I know you don't really like that I have a history with Sofia, but I do. And I can't change it. But, Cooper, please understand, I'd give up this house a hundred times over if it means I get to keep my life as it is now. It's kind of perfect."

He smiled at me. "That's because I'm in it."

I rolled my eyes at his way of making everything about him. Even if it was.

"It's funny," he said thoughtfully. "I mean, I can see how, fifteen years ago, this was the perfect holiday home for a family. I can see that. But it's big, and I don't know…" He trailed off. "But what bothers me is that this house," he said with a sigh, "this house isn't the Tom I know."

"The house isn't me?"

He shook his head, looking around the room. "No, I don't know *this* Tom."

"You mean you didn't know me fifteen years ago when I designed it?"

"Yeah, I'm probably not explaining it right," he said. "It's just not what I would see you in now, if you designed something to suit your life as it is now. The Tom that I know."

"What do you think I would design?"

"Something smaller. Earthier. With more wood and stone. Something more rustic, not the vast open spaces this place has. More cabin-like, with a fire and a small marble kitchen. I just see you in something more honest and genuine, no pretenses."

I smiled and shook my head slowly. "You read me so well."

"I know you," he said simply. "And there would be a room like a study or an attic, with a wall of glass or dormer windows for the telescope and a drawing board where you would get lost for hours."

"Well that's where you're wrong," I whispered.

He tilted his head and raised one eyebrow in question.

"There would be *two* drawing boards."

Cooper smiled and ducked his head, almost shyly. "Yes, there would."

I walked over to him and kissed him. "It still amazes me how much you see the real me."

He exhaled contentedly. "I am kind of awesome like that."

"Yes, you are," I said, before kissing him again. "Why don't you get some work done while I work my culinary magic in the kitchen."

Cooper raised a sarcastic eyebrow at me. "Culinary magic?"

"Oh, shut up," I grumbled. "I suck at cooking and you know it."

He had a glazed, dreamy look on his face, and after a while, he said, "I'm sorry, you mentioned sucking and I got distracted. I didn't hear a word after that." I rolled my eyes and walked into the kitchen, but he called out, "Your cooking is fine, Tom. But your sucking skills are your true talent."

I ignored his comment and set about getting a dinner ready while Cooper got lost in his paperwork and laptop. As I chopped and diced, I thought about what Cooper had said.

It made total sense. Then again, most of what he said did.

This house, the Casa, was big, purpose-built for a family. Large open spaces, and maybe there was a detached feeling to that, which Cooper had picked up on. Maybe there was a detached feeling to the man who had designed it all those years ago.

I loved how he said this house wasn't the Tom he knew.

I loved how he could identify the architect with a building but then differentiate them as well.

He knew me so damn well. We'd not even been together a year, and yet he knew things about me I didn't even know.

"You'd better be thinking of me when you smile like that," Cooper said, now standing beside me.

I hadn't heard him come into the kitchen. I bumped his hip with mine. "Of course I'm thinking about you."

"Then why aren't you hard?" he asked, looking pointedly at my crotch. Before I could say anything, he said, "They have pills now, for old guys who can't get hard."

I pointed a carrot at him. "I can get hard just fine," I said. "You know that damn well... unless you need reminding?"

Cooper leaned forward and bit the end off the carrot. He grinned and waggled his eyebrows, as if he was daring me. "I think I might need reminding." He chewed the mouthful of carrot and swallowed. "But dinner first. I'm starving."

After dinner, Cooper went back to work while I cleaned up. And by the time I fell onto the sofa, Cooper shut down his laptop and shuffled in beside me. We watched some TV, and even though I finally got him to relax and have some downtime, I could tell he wasn't too comfortable in the Casa.

Not that he was *un*comfortable, just not his usual vibrant self. I think it was because it reminded him that I'd had a life before him. I'd shared this house, the bedroom upstairs, with Sofia...

"Oh, Jesus," I groaned. "I shouldn't have brought you here."

Cooper sat up and stared at me, confusion clear on his face. "What? Why not?" His voice was quiet and worried. Oh, God. He thought I didn't want him here.

"No, I didn't mean it like that," I said quickly, taking his hand. "I just meant that I don't want to be in this house. You were right. I don't like what it represents, my life with Sofia, and I shouldn't have expected you to stay here."

"Tom..."

I shook my head. "I didn't even think of it like that, until just now. I didn't mean to bring you to a place that reminds you of me with someone else."

"Tom?"

"Come on," I said, standing up. "We'll find a hotel or just drive back to the city."

"Tom!" Cooper said, louder this time. He pulled me back onto the sofa beside him. "It's fine. We don't have to leave." Then he leaned up and swung one leg over me, so he was straddling me. He pushed me back into the backrest of the sofa and looked down at me. He softly planted his lips on mine. "But maybe you needed to come here one more time, so when we leave tomorrow it will be like a final good-bye... to this part of your life."

"It will be, yes," I whispered. I leaned up and kissed him. "It's kind of fitting that you're here with me, actually."

He smiled and nodded. "So we don't have to leave?"

I shook my head slowly. "If you want to stay, we'll stay."

"Good. I want you to take me to bed. Last time we were here, we fooled around, but we didn't really get to christen the bed properly. I was too drunk at Ryan's party, if I remember correctly," he said. His eyes sparked with mischief. "So I think we better do it twice tonight to make up for it."

"Is that so?"

Cooper nodded. Then he was serious. "Thank you for thinking of me," he said. He pecked my lips with his own. "I'm lucky to have you."

"I was just thinking the same thing."

"Take me upstairs, Tom," he said. "I don't think Sofia would appreciate stains on her sofa."

I did as he asked, of course. Then he did the same to me.

THE NEXT MORNING, we took a long walk on the beach. It was getting cool, and Cooper tucked himself into my side as we walked. He talked of the project he was working on with Xavier and how the job was moving along nicely. He seemed content to just talk, and I could listen to him forever.

He was even okay when I called in quickly to see my mom. He walked in, smiled as he said hello, and politely accepted the offer of coffee. Mom was doing okay—she missed Dad terribly and said she always would, but I wanted to check in on her, considering we weren't too far away.

My mom was pleasant enough, she wouldn't ever be rude to Cooper, but she also didn't acknowledge our relationship. I doubted she probably ever would. But she knew I was gay, she knew I was with him, she simply chose to not talk about it. And that was okay.

When we'd said goodbye and were on our way back to the city, Cooper sighed contentedly. "You know, I think your mom is starting to warm to me."

"How so?"

"She offered me coffee," he said with a smile. "She doesn't have to start any new PFLAG chapters or anything, but she smiled when she saw you, and she offered me coffee. That's pretty lucky."

I took his hand over the center console. "I was just thinking the same thing. She'll probably never say the word 'gay' or 'boyfriend,' but as long as she smiles and offers us coffee, then we're good."

Then right on cue, Cooper's cell phone rang. He checked the screen before answering. "Mom?"

I watched the road, but I could hear his mother's voice through the phone.

"Um, two weeks?" Cooper said. "Hang on, I'll check." He put the phone against his chest so his mom couldn't hear. "Mom wants to come to New York in two weeks, just for the weekend. Is that okay?"

"Of course it is, you don't need to ask me," I said.

Cooper smiled and lifted the phone back to his ear. "Sure, Mom. Weekend after next would be great."

After a short conversation, he disconnected the call and smiled. It was obvious the offer for a visit was one of acceptance. "There's some show Mom wants to see," he said, still smiling. "Thought it would be a great excuse to come for a visit."

"That's great, Cooper." I took his hand again, giving it a squeeze. "You know my apartment's yours now too, you live there. You don't have to ask permission for anyone to stay. Your entire family is welcome."

"Good," he said with a grin. "Because my entire family is coming."

CHAPTER SIX

WORK THAT WEEK WAS HECTIC, as per usual. Cooper's was even busier than mine. He was hoping to wrap up the job with Xavier soon and was putting in the hours to get it done.

I couldn't say I blamed him. Xavier Baurhenn was a jerk, and Cooper was fed up with him.

Cooper was really looking forward to his family visiting, and truth be told, as much as it made me nervous, it was a positive step forward. Cooper needed them in his life. He wanted their approval, whether he admitted it or not, and I wanted him to be happy. So we were planning a dinner at home on Saturday night, hoping they'd see Cooper was still the same.

The weekend before his parents were due to visit, he'd taken a break from work and decided he was going to cook for the dinner party. He had the menu planned and everything. The only thing he wanted my help with was to choose the wine, but then he proceeded to tell me which types of wine his parents preferred, so he ended up taking that task off me as well.

Sitting at the dining table, he was writing lists and recipes, while I watched on in wonder. He was a control freak, through and through. "Cooper, sweetheart," I said with a kiss to his temple. "They're coming here to see you, which shows they're making an effort."

"Which is why it has to be perfect!" he cried.

"It will be. Just be yourself."

He exhaled through puffed-out cheeks. "Tom, I just want them to see *us*, you know?"

"They will," I reassured him.

"How come you're so confident?"

"Because they love you," I answered. "And because you're cooking, not me."

He finally smiled. "That's true."

I snatched the shopping list. "At least let me get the groceries."

Cooper smiled at me. "You mean, let Jennifer order them for you."

I resisted sticking my tongue out at him. "Jennifer doesn't do *everything* for me."

His lips twisted as he tried not to smile. "Oh, okay, if you say so," he said, rolling his eyes. "Tell her it doesn't matter what kind of flowers she orders, just as long as they're bright."

I didn't even try to deny that I'd be giving the list to Jennifer. I lifted my chin with dignity. "Jennifer knows where to buy the best stuff."

Cooper laughed. "So, if the day ever arrives when I get flowers delivered, or cool Lego sets, or new Prada boots from the new winter collection, I'll just presume Jennifer buys them for me?"

This time it was me who laughed. "New Prada boots?"

"Well, they *are* nice," he lamented. "They're black and

pull-on, and they have this stitching patterned across the toe... you know, just in case you were wondering which ones..."

I shook my head at him. "Your ability to drop a subtle hint is sorely lacking."

Cooper got up from his seat, sat himself on my lap, and kissed me. "You know what else is sorely lacking?"

I smiled. "No idea."

"You."

I quirked an eyebrow at him. "Me?"

"I've been so busy, and I feel so bad, and this week will be even busier, and then next week my family will be here," he said. "I don't want you to feel like you're second place for me, because you're not." He held my face in his hands. "You're first place, all the time. Even if I'm at work, or in a meeting, or whatever, you're always first."

His words and the sincerity in his eyes made me smile. "I know that."

"I know you say you understand how busy I am, but, Tom, I can't see it slowing down anytime soon, and if anything, the more my name gets out there, the busier I'll be."

"Cooper, it's fine, really."

"You say that now. But what about later, in a year or five years' time, when you're sick of being alone?"

"I won't be alone," I told him. "I have my work, too. And Ryan, and my mom—and, Cooper, I have you. We'll just have to plan around our schedules and work in some time for us."

He smiled. "I'd like that. Maybe one weekend a month we could take off. Get out of the city, or book a mystery flight away for a few days every now and then, or even if we stay here, we can tell Lionel we've gone, turn our phones off, and block out the world."

"That sounds perfect."

"I just don't want to lose us. Life's gonna get busy, and I want to keep us in check, you know?"

I kissed him sweetly. "God, I love you. You're just..."

"Awesome?"

"Sassy."

"Did you just call me a little shit?"

I shook my head slowly. "Maybe."

"And to think I was going to ask you to take me to bed." He sighed dramatically. "Now I might just insist on you cooking me dinner."

"How about both?"

"In what order?"

"Does it matter?"

"Yes."

"How hungry are you?"

"Starving."

"How about I order dinner to be delivered, which should give us about forty minutes to fill in."

He smiled when he kissed me. "I do believe I like the way you think."

FIRST CHANCE I got at work on Monday, I googled Prada stores, then the boots he had mentioned. One thing was certain. Cooper had expensive taste. Whether he was joking about wanting the boots or not, I had to admit, they did look good.

But then knowing ordering them online wouldn't be

good enough, I went to the store during my lunch hour. I had the store wrap them and courier them to his office with a handwritten note attached that read, *Anything for you...*

I got sidetracked with new clientele, and it wasn't until I was walking home that I realized I'd not heard from Cooper. I was a little disappointed but looked forward to seeing his reaction first-hand when he got home.

It was late, well after I'd gotten home, and he walked through the door looking tired. He slumped his messenger bag on the floor next to the sofa, then sat across from me on the other sofa. I put the job file I was reading through down and watched him.

Without a word, he lifted his newly-Prada-booted feet and slid them onto the coffee table, and a slow smile spread across his face. "Anything for you," he repeated what I'd written on the card.

I stared straight at him. "Yes."

"You didn't have to actually buy them, you know. I was only joking."

"Your wish, my command. Or something like that," I said, smiling back at him.

"My wish?"

"I believe I said anything, yes."

"My wish is you, in me."

My eyes widened at his blatant request. "Is that so?"

"Yes."

"You're very tired."

"Then fuck me slowly."

I shook my head at him, but stood up and held out my hand. He took it, and I pulled him to his feet but as I stepped toward the hall, he pulled me back to him. Cooper slid his arms around me and held me, nuzzling into my neck.

"I was having such a shitty day today," he mumbled into my collarbone. "And then I got some boots delivered and you have no idea how much I wanted to leave right then and come see you."

I tightened my hold on him and ran one hand over the back of his head.

"It wasn't even the boots, really." Then he amended, "Don't get me wrong. They're great, but the card..."

"Anything for you," I whispered against the side of his head.

He nodded. "It was just what I needed to hear. Thank you."

"You're very welcome."

"Take me to bed, Tom."

"You're so tired, sweetheart."

He pulled back to look at me. "Are you going to make me beg?"

I shook my head and kissed his lips. "Never."

I made love to him, softly, slowly. I savored every movement, every thrust. Cooper was on his back, with his legs bent to his chest. He never took his mouth from mine. He kissed me deeply, keeping rhythm with every roll of my hips. His orgasm surged through him, his eyes fluttered closed, and his fingers dug into my skin.

By the time I had us both cleaned up, he was half asleep. When I crawled in next to him, he burrowed himself into my side. I kissed the side of his head and whispered that I loved him, but he was already asleep.

TUESDAY AT WORK WAS PRODUCTIVE. I got in

early, left late and got a lot of work done. Jennifer came in just before she left for the day and sat down across from me. She looked worried.

"Tom," she said. "Robert's up to something."

I put my pen down and sighed. "What do you mean?"

"He's been asking questions around the office, apparently. Not just on this floor either. I don't know what his problem is."

"His problem is that I'm gay," I told her outright.

"He never had a problem with it before."

"He never saw me with anyone before," I said. "I'm presuming when he saw me with Cooper at my father's funeral, he didn't like it much."

"He never said anything to me," she told me. "He sat with me the entire time."

I shrugged. "It's the only thing I can think of."

"Well, I don't like it, Tom. It makes me feel uneasy." She shook her head. "You've given so much of your life to this place. I just don't know what he's trying to achieve."

"Maybe he wants me gone."

Jennifer blinked. "I work for you. I don't want to work for anyone else."

I gave her a smile. "I'm sure it won't come to that. He simply can't just say he wants me fired because I'm gay. He'd be in court faster than he could blink, and he knows it. I gave him the perfect opportunity to issue me with a written notice, citing violation of policy, and he didn't do it."

"Because he couldn't prove anything."

"That was just him letting me know he knew damn well I'd breached policy," I told her. I exhaled loudly. "Jennifer, I don't know, to be honest. But as long as I keep doing my job, he can't say anything. He might not like my choice of partner, but it doesn't concern him."

Jennifer frowned. "Well, I don't like it."

I gave her a smile. "I know, but try not to worry. It'll be fine, you'll see."

She gave me a nod, though she hardly looked convinced. "Give Cooper my best."

"I will," I told her. "I'll just wrap up this file and be heading home myself."

"See you in the morning," she said, and the door closed quietly behind her.

Needless to say, my mind was hardly on the job folder in front of me.

Whatever Robert's issues were, they were with me, and I hated that Jennifer was worried over whatever nonsense he was hell-bent on proving.

I'd given ten years of my life to Brackett and Golding. I'd worked seven days a week, putting in countless, endless hours. I'd won contract after contract, award after award— they were on shelves and walls, peppering my success in this company over the last decade.

Admittedly, the success was for me as much as it was for Brackett and Golding. But the feeling of being shunned, ousted, was not pleasant.

Actually, it was pretty fucking awful.

I packed up my briefcase, needing to talk to Cooper. I knew it would piss him off and that I had to tell him, but it was late when he got home. He was stressed enough with the Xavier job and his parents visiting this weekend, so I tried to let it go.

But when we were lying in bed, with Cooper's head on my chest, me tracing circles on his back, I had to tell him. I didn't want to keep anything from him. I took a deep breath and said, "I think Robert's trying to get rid of me."

He leaned up on his elbow. "Seriously?"

I nodded. "Yeah."

He opened his mouth, no doubt to rant, but I rolled onto my side and faced him. "Cooper, don't worry. I haven't been issued any kind of warning or anything like that. He's just been snooping, trying to find something that will stick. Nothing may come of it. I just wanted you to know."

Even in the darkened room, I could see him frown. "What's his problem? Is it me? Is it because I was your intern? Is it something you did? Is it something I did?"

I traced my fingers across his cheekbone. "I think it's because I'm gay."

Cooper's mouth snapped shut, and I knew he was mad. So I leaned in and kissed him, soft and sweet. "Cooper, sweetheart, I've told you before. I wouldn't change a thing I've done. I wouldn't. I don't care what he thinks, or anyone else for that matter. He can fire me for all I care, because I somehow got you. And I'd choose you every day for the rest of my life over Robert Chandler."

Cooper fell onto his back. "Jesus, Tom. Don't ask me to marry you when I'm mad. Fuck."

I laughed and pulled him against me. "Was there a proposal in there somewhere, on some Cooper frequency that I didn't hear?"

He sighed. "You keep talking forever."

I nodded. "And marriage and forever are the same?"

"Yep."

I kissed the top of his head, unable to stop smiling. "Go to sleep."

He mumbled, "Don't tell me what to do," but tightened his hold on me, and soon was sound asleep.

I WENT about my work on Wednesday, like any other day. I kept an eye out for Robert but didn't see him. Cooper called me after lunch to see how things were, and I told him it was all just normal. "Maybe I'm imagining it," I said.

"And Jennifer?" he asked. "She doesn't miss a thing in that office."

I sighed. "She's the one who told me she thought something was wrong."

"Fuck, Tom," he said with a groan.

"We'll talk about it tonight."

"I'll be late." He sighed. "I'm so close to finishing this, and then Xavier Baurhenn will be out of my life."

"I'll wait up."

"You better."

I smiled as I hung up the phone. But we didn't talk about it when he got home.

The doctor called him at work with his blood test results, and we talked about that instead. Everything was clear, and physically he was in perfect health. But he was unsure about something. He was leaning against the kitchen counter, frowning.

"Cooper, what is it?"

He shrugged. "Well, just about the unprotected sex conversation we had before..."

"We don't have to not use condoms," I said. "Like we said before, no pressure. When we're ready."

"I want to," he said quietly. "Not yet, I don't think. But one day, soon maybe, if you want..."

I lifted his chin and kissed his lips. "I want to, but when we're ready."

He bit his lip and nodded. "Okay."

"No pressure," I added. "We'll know when it's the right time."

His stomach grumbled, interrupting the conversation. I insisted he eat something, which he did, then I ran us a steaming hot shower and we fell into bed where he made love to me.

It was slow and deep, and when I imagined what it would be like to one day have him inside me, condomless, skin on skin, how he'd come inside me, I came.

ON THURSDAY MORNING, we walked through the lobby saying a quick hello to Lionel and chatting about New York winters. Cooper had reminded me of the grocery order I had to make today for his parents' dinner party. "Oh, and the little Italian patisserie on Eighth has these little fig tarts. I'm sure Mrs. Lionel would love them heated up."

Lionel was quick to object, "No, Mr. Jones, you don't have to do that."

"I don't," Cooper replied simply. "Tom does."

Lionel looked at me, somewhat alarmed, and I just smiled and rolled my eyes. "Really, Lionel, there is no point in arguing."

Lionel gave me a smile and a shrug, and Cooper nodded like his work here was done. With a quick kiss, Cooper and I went our separate ways to work.

My morning was uneventful, but just before my ten o'clock meeting, Jennifer buzzed through my intercom. "Mr. Elkin?"

She sounded worried. "What is it, Jennifer?"

"You have a phone call on line one. He said his name was Lionel."

I frowned at the blinking button on my phone. "Thanks,

Jennifer. I'll take it." I picked up the receiver. "Thomas Elkin speaking."

"Mr. Elkin," Lionel's familiar voice said.

"Lionel, is everything okay?"

"Well, yes," he said, unsure. "I've tried calling Mr. Jones, but he's in meetings all day, apparently. I hope you don't mind me calling you at work. I have your office number in case of emergencies."

"Lionel, it's fine," I said, knowing he'd never call me if it wasn't warranted. "What is it?"

"There's a young gentleman here who says he's here to see Mr. Jones. He says his name is Maxwell Jones. He says he's Mr. Jones' brother?"

"Max?"

"Yes, sir." Then Lionel said, "I don't want to send him out onto the streets, Mr. Elkin, if he is indeed Mr. Jones' brother."

"Does he have long black hair, a nose ring?"

"Yes, sir."

Shit. "Tell him to wait. I'll be there in ten minutes."

CHAPTER SEVEN

WHEN I WALKED into the lobby of my apartment, Lionel was laughing with our surprise visitor, who was indeed Max.

Cooper's brother's eyes brightened when he saw me. Whether he was just happy to see a familiar face or me in particular, I wasn't sure. Considering I'd only met him once and he'd called me old, I assumed it was the former.

"Hey," Max said, by way of greeting. His longish black hair hung over half his face.

"Hey," I replied as casually as I could. "We were expecting you tomorrow. Cooper never said you were coming a day early."

"Oh, he doesn't know I'm here." Max shrugged as though it was no big deal.

"Max," I said, using my talking-to-teenagers voice. "Do your parents know you're here?"

"Yeah. I told them Coop knew I was coming, but I just forgot to call him. I was gonna call him from the airport, but then I forgot." He looked me up and down, seeing I was wearing a suit. "Oh, man. Did you leave work?"

I smiled at him, considering it was just after ten in the morning on a workday. "Ah, yes."

I glanced at Lionel then, and it prompted him to speak. "Max here was just telling me about his flight." The crinkles around his eyes deepened when he smiled. "They don't look much alike, but they're definitely brothers."

I smiled a little more genuinely then. He wasn't just some seventeen-year-old kid. He was Cooper's brother. Then I noticed a backpack near his feet. "Come on, we'll take your things upstairs."

Max picked up his bag, and as we headed toward the elevator, I turned back and gave a nod of thanks to Lionel. He gave a knowing smile in return. As we took the elevator to my apartment, I wondered what the fucking hell I was supposed to do with a seventeen-year-old kid.

"Hey, sorry to be a pain in the ass," Max said.

I wasn't even sure if I should be correcting his language. I decided no, it wasn't my place. "It's okay." I let us into the apartment. "You can put your bag in the spare room. First door on your left down the hall, bathroom is the second door. I'll just try calling Cooper."

Max disappeared and I pulled out my cell. Of course he didn't answer. Twice. So I called his office, something I really didn't like doing. A bright and cheerful female voice answered, only to tell me Cooper was out on the job site and would be back in another hour or two.

Shit. Shit, shit, shit.

Since I couldn't very well leave him in the apartment by himself, the next number I dialed was my office. Jennifer answered promptly. I told her I wouldn't be back in today. I had two appointments this afternoon and told Jennifer one of my team could sit in on my behalf and fill me in later.

Then it occurred to me that Cooper would be even

busier tomorrow, trying to get everything finalized on the Baurhenn job, so I told Jennifer to clear my schedule for tomorrow as well, just in case.

As I clicked off the call to Jennifer, Max walked back out and was looking around the living room. He inspected the photos, the antique drafting board, then the Lego Sydney Opera House, but before he could touch it, I said, "Max, Cooper won't be back for a few hours."

He stared at me from behind his half-wall of hair. "Oh."

"So you're stuck with me."

"You don't need to babysit me."

I rolled my eyes at the very Cooper remark. "I'm hardly babysitting. Been to New York before?"

"Not since I was a kid."

"Well then," I said. "Where did you want to go first?"

Max smiled. "Really?"

"Just let me get changed," I said, but then stopped halfway to my room. "As long as it's not some death-metal concert crap. It's bad enough I have to listen to Cooper's taste in music, and I won't be responsible for tattoos. You do that with Cooper, not me."

Max grinned at me. "Deal *and* deal."

I quickly dressed in jeans and a light jacket and suggested we go get some lunch. As we sat and ate, we made small talk and I learned a few things about him—he had a girlfriend called Ashley, she had pink hair and liked a list of bands I'd never heard of. At first appearances, Max didn't look like Cooper, at all. But underneath the dyed black hair and silver ring through his face, they were a lot alike.

They both had curious, keen eyes, a sense of self, and strong opinions. I smiled when Max said he wanted to go to the University of Illinois and study computer science.

"There's a science of computers?" I asked.

He looked at me like I'd sprouted a second head. "It's programming and software design."

"So, you're exceptionally smart?"

He smiled at that. "I'm a four-point-oh."

He looked like a goth-wannabe kid with attitude, but he wasn't that way at all. "So the clothes, the hair, the nose ring?"

"Just part of my awesomeness."

I burst out laughing. "Oh, my God. You are so much like your brother."

Max chuckled quietly but shrugged one shoulder. "Never really thought about it."

"You and Cooper both have to know how things work, yes?"

Max half shrugged. "I guess." Then he added, "When we were younger, he'd build stuff and I'd watch. I wasn't allowed to play with his Lego," he said with a roll of his eyes. "But he was older than me, so he'd build houses and buildings and castles..."

"And what did you do?"

"I watched him. Sometimes I'd play with his stuff when he wasn't there, so he wouldn't know," Max said with a grin. "When he got older, all he wanted to do was draw. He did graphic arts and shit like that. Went from building houses to drawing 'em."

"And you like computers?"

He nodded and sipped his Coke. "Yep. It's just what I know. Natural progression from playing games to designing them," he said simply.

"You design computer games?" I couldn't hide my surprise.

One corner of his lip curled up into the same smug smile Cooper had. "Only basic ones, but yep.

Working on more complicated programming, but it takes time."

I smiled knowingly. They were so alike. Not in looks, but personality-wise they were. And more obviously, they were both very smart, and both designers, creators. It was kind of remarkable. "Maybe one day you can create a design program for architects to make our jobs a bit easier."

"Nah, not really my scene." Max pushed the rest of his uneaten lunch away. "I'm thinking more along the lines of the next Google or Windows."

I laughed. "Nothing like aiming high."

"Go hard or go home, right?"

"You're so much like Cooper," I said, shaking my head. "Come on, let's go see if he's back in his office."

We started walking the three blocks to Cooper's office and I pointed out a few buildings of interest. Max wasn't particularly enthralled but nodded just to be polite, I was sure.

He and Cooper definitely didn't share a love of architecture.

I'd only been to Cooper's office a couple of times, and only ever on a weekend when it was all but empty, but I knew which floor he was on. Getting out of the elevator and facing Arlington reception, we were greeted by a woman I'd not seen before.

"Can I help you?"

"I'd like to see Cooper Jones, please," I said giving her my most pleasant smile.

She tapped on her keyboard. "Is he expecting you?"

"Well, no actually, he's not," I explained. "But if you tell him Tom is here"—I looked at Max—"and a surprise."

Max spoke then, "He's Tom, I'm the surprise," he said with a disarming grin. God, he was so like Cooper.

"I'm afraid you'll need to make an appointment..." she started to tell me.

I put my hand up. "Never mind, thank you." I pulled my cell phone out and pressed redial.

Cooper answered on the second ring. "Hey."

"Hey," I replied. "I'm in reception."

"Where?"

"At your office," I explained. "In reception. I have... something for you." I looked at Max and smiled.

"Is it a matching Prada leather jacket?" he asked, but I could hear he was walking as he talked. "Because they have these black jackets with these tags and buckles. They're incredible."

"No, it's not a matching Prada jacket," I said, rolling my eyes.

Max smiled.

"Is it two tickets to Muse?"

"No, it's certainly not," I answered, wondering how long it would take and how long the list was of possible gifts he was giving me hints for.

"Tickets to Paris?"

"Are you even in the building? Because this list is getting more expensive the longer I wait."

He laughed, but I heard him down the hallway rather than through the phone. Cooper appeared at the door, and his smile died, his eyes widened.

"Max?"

"Surprise," Max said flatly, almost sarcastically.

Cooper crossed the floor and hugged his brother. "What are you doing here? Are Mom and Dad here?" Then he looked at me, then back to Max. "Why are you with Tom?"

"I came a day early. Mom and Dad aren't here. I flew in this morning."

Cooper blinked. "You came to New York City? By yourself? Are you insane? You're seventeen! What the hell were Mom and Dad thinking?"

"Well... well, they thought you organized it..."

That was news to me as well. Cooper's face paled. "Max, do they even know you're here?"

Max looked at me, then back to Cooper. "Yeah... they... Well..."

Cooper grabbed Max's arm and led him down the hallway he'd just walked out of. I smiled at the receptionist, who was watching in wide-eyed wonder. I gave her a smile. "Brothers."

I followed Cooper and Max down the hall to Cooper's working station. The Arlington offices were an open-floor area, with communal tables and spaces which apparently encouraged teamwork and brainstorming. They were all about pushing boundaries on modernization and contemporary planning and design. It was... exciting.

It was so different from Brackett and Golding.

In all honesty, I preferred my private office. I did like working alone. But the concept, the enterprise of Arlington, was definitely modern and would lead the direction of where architecture was going. It reminded me that I'd made the right decision in calling Louisa Arlington to get Cooper an interview here.

Cooper led Max into a conference room, and I followed them in.

"Sit your ass in a chair," Cooper barked at his brother. At the same time, he had his cell phone out and to his ear, waiting for whoever he was calling to answer. "I can't believe you just turned up here. I can't believe you came here on your own!" Then he spoke into the phone. "Hi, Mom, yeah, it's Cooper. Give me a call."

Cooper clicked off the call and exhaled loudly, and finally looked at me. Seeing I was dressed casually, he said, "I'm not even sure how you're with him, but I'm grateful. And I'm sorry. Jesus, Max. A little warning next time."

"I was going to call," Max said. "But then I got busy, then I forgot, and then I was going to call from the airport but I forgot."

"It's okay, Cooper," I said. "Lionel said he tried calling you a few times this morning, but you didn't answer, so he called me instead. I don't mind, really."

Cooper shook his head. "But you're so busy, and I was out all morning. I'm trying to get this Baurhenn job finished by tomorrow... Oh my God, tomorrow..." He looked at his brother. "Crap. I can't take tomorrow off, I'm totally swamped."

"I can look after myself," Max said. "I don't need a babysitter."

Cooper raised one eyebrow and pursed his lips. "You are not walking around New York City by yourself."

"Jeez, Coop," Max said, rolling his eyes. "Gettin' your Dad voice on."

I chuckled at that. His biting, sarcastic comments were so much like his brother's. "Cooper, it's fine. I've already told Jennifer I won't be in tomorrow."

"You can't have two days off!"

I scoffed. "I've had a total of four weeks off in about ten years. I'm sure I'm entitled to two days' family time. Anyway," I added, "I'm kind of glad not to be there right now."

Cooper frowned. "Oh, Tom. I'm sorry. I know you're having a shitty time at work right now, and I wish I wasn't so damn busy. I'm not being much help right now, am I?"

"Max and I are fine," I reassured him. "I'm sure we'll find something he wants to do."

Max spun himself around in the swivel chair. "As long as it doesn't involve thrash metal or getting tattoos. Those are Tom's rules."

Cooper looked at me. "Rules?"

I shrugged one shoulder. "Thought they were fair."

Cooper stared at me for a long moment, as though trying to think of the right thing to say. Then he sighed. "Thank you."

I smiled back at him. "You're very welcome."

"Ugh," Max groaned. "You two finished with the heart-eyes? Because no one should see their brother getting it on."

"Hey," Cooper said, pointing his finger at his brother. But before he could start ranting, his cell phone rang. He growled as he answered the call. "Hello... Oh, hi, Mom." Cooper pulled a face at his brother. "Yeah, he's here, safe and sound."

Max pulled a face back at Cooper. Cooper tried to swipe Max's face. Max ducked and softly jabbed at Cooper's ribs. "Yeah, of course, he asked me. We had it all lined up... Okay, we'll call you later."

Cooper disconnected the call and stared at Max. "I just lied to our mother to cover your ass." He shook his head and exhaled through puffed-out cheeks. Then he and Max stared at each other until they started to smile. "Come on, I'll show you my desk."

Cooper held the door open for us. Max walked out first, and when I got to the door, Cooper quickly ran his hand over my back and pecked my cheek. "Love you."

I smiled and told him what he always tells me. "I know you do. It's because I'm awesome."

Cooper laughed, and for the next ten minutes or so,

Cooper showed Max his workstation. Max was more interested in the computer system, of course, and spoke in some foreign binary language I couldn't follow. I just stood back, leaning against the wall to let them have some time, albeit brief time, together.

I didn't even notice a group of people approaching until they walked past. Then they stopped. And stared at me.

There were three of them—two men and one woman, all about the same age as Cooper or a bit older.

"Oh my God. You're Thomas Elkin?" one of the men said. The other guy was wide-eyed and the woman slack-jawed.

I leaned off the wall and extended my hand. "Yes, I am. How are you?"

By the time I'd introduced myself to the three of them, Cooper, and Max, some others at the other end of the large office space were watching us.

"What are you doing here?" the first guy asked. "Are you overseeing something?" Then his eyes brightened. "A collaboration with Arlington?"

The three of them waited eagerly, and a silence fell across the room waiting for my reply. Luckily it was lunchtime and half the room was empty. "Uh, no. I'm just here with Cooper," I said, giving a pointed nod to him.

All eyes went to Cooper, who opened his mouth to say something, but it was Max who laughed. "Is Tom like some kind of celebrity or something?"

I laughed at that, and Cooper blushed and mumbled, "No, he's just Tom."

One of the three people, I think it was the woman, whispered, "Just Tom?"

I nodded and told them, "It's true. I am just Tom." By this time, Cooper had pulled Max away from his desk, leading him toward the door. But then he stopped and faced his coworkers who were all now watching us.

"Everyone, this is my brother, Max," he said, waving his hand in introduction. "And my partner, Tom Elkin."

I waved my hand. "Hi."

I got a collective shocked, mumbled response, and Cooper turned on his heel and Max and I followed him out. I felt bad because I knew only a select few of Cooper's coworkers had known about me. "I'm sorry," I said. "I did try to call."

Cooper shook his head. "No, don't apologize. They were all bound to find out sooner or later." He looked back to the way we'd come. "I'm about to get a gazillion questions." Then he looked at Max. "You behave yourself. And here, take my credit card," he said, pulling out his wallet. "Don't let Tom buy you anything."

Then Cooper looked at me. "I'm so sorry. I promise I'll make it up to you."

We said goodbye, and when we walked back out onto the New York City sidewalk, Max burst out laughing. "Oh my God, that was funny," he said. "You're like someone famous or something?"

"Only to those who know architecture."

Max grinned. "Okay then, Mr. Ce-leb-rity, what are we doing now?"

"Something awesome."

"If you say 'because that's how you roll,' I'm boarding the next plane back to Chicago."

I barked out a laugh. "You're so much like your freakin' brother."

CHAPTER EIGHT

WHEN COOPER GOT HOME, I was in the kitchen cleaning up after dinner. He dropped his messenger bag at the door and without a word to his brother, he walked up to me and slid his arms around my waist. I threw the dishcloth into the sink and hugged him back. His face was buried in my neck and he mumbled, "Thank you, Tom. For everything."

"You're very welcome," I whispered back to him. "Have you eaten?"

Without pulling away, he shook his head. "No."

"We ordered pizza. Max said Chicago pizzas were the best, so I thought we'd have proper New York pizza just to prove him wrong," I said. "I got your favorite."

Cooper gave me a squeeze. "You're so good to me."

"Coop?" Max said. He was now standing in the kitchen beside us, not seeming to care that Cooper was still wrapped around me. Max was still excited. He'd been waiting for his brother to get home. "You'll never believe where Tom took me this afternoon."

Cooper pulled away then, to look at me, then to Max. "Where?"

I took out a plate and put some pizza in the microwave for Cooper, as Max said, "First stop was Academy Records. Best vinyl album shop; they have all this vintage stuff. It was really cool. Then we went to Café Wha?."

"Café where?"

"No, Café Wha?," he repeated. "Where Jimi Hendrix played! We couldn't go in because I'm seventeen, but Cooper, we went to where Jimi Hendrix played!"

Cooper was smiling at Max's enthusiasm. "That's so cool!"

"But then," Max said. "The best place ever... Tom took me to Generation Records."

Cooper blinked, then his eyes darted to mine and back to Max's. "And that's cool because...?"

"Because it's the best metal and punk record store ever. Like, ever. If it's metal or punk, they have it," Max said. "Coop, it was so freakin' cool."

I handed Cooper his reheated pizza. "I am officially the coolest guy on the planet."

Cooper took the plate and stared at me. "You really took him there?"

"I did."

Cooper took a step closer and planted his lips on mine. "Thank you." Then he looked at Max. "Did my credit card survive?"

Max laughed. "Yeah, yeah. But I bought you something, so that makes it okay."

"With my own money. How thoughtful of you." Cooper took a bite of pizza and spoke with his mouth full, "So where is it?"

"Well, Tom picked it," Max admitted. "I said I wanted to get you something cool, so Tom found you this..." Max walked over to the sofa and picked up the bag and held it out proudly.

Cooper followed him over to the sofa, put his plate on the coffee table and threw himself onto the sofa. Max handed him the shopping bag and we watched as he pulled out a Ramones CD and a Sex Pistols shirt.

"Oh, man," Cooper said quietly. "Did you pick these?" he asked me.

"Yep. I figured the Ramones were easier to listen to than the Sex Pistols, plus I liked the shirt. Well, for you. Not for me."

Cooper held up the white, sleeveless shirt with a washed-out Union Jack Flag on it and the anarchy A. "I love it." Cooper took another mouthful of pizza and started to unbutton his shirt.

Max looked at Cooper. "Dude. What are you doing?"

"I'm gonna wear my new shirt," he answered.

"Thank God I didn't buy you the briefs."

"Did they have Sex Pistols undies? Because I would totally wear those," Cooper said seriously. He grabbed his slice of pizza and sat back down on the sofa.

I laughed, leaned over the back of the sofa, and kissed the side of his head. "I'll leave you two to chat. I'm going to our bedroom to check emails and catch up on the critical stuff I missed today."

Cooper stood up. "Are you sure? Tom, you can stay out here."

I walked back over to him and kissed him. "I'm sure. You two can catch up. I can get some work done," I said. "Plus, I walked the entire length of the city today. I could put my feet up for a while. I'm old, remember?"

Cooper rolled his eyes but put his hand on my chest. "Okay. I won't be too long. I'm tired, myself."

I looked at Max. "Thanks for a good day. I had fun."

"Thank *you*," Max said. "Can't wait to see what we're doing tomorrow."

I groaned at the thought and left them to it. As I walked down the hall, I heard Max say, "He's not, you know."

"He's not what?" Cooper asked warily.

"Old," Max answered. "He said he wanted to put his feet up because he's old. But he's not."

"I know that," Cooper said. It sounded like he was smiling.

"He's pretty cool actually," Max said.

Cooper laughed. "Yeah, I know that."

Smiling, I shut the door quietly and left them to it. They could use some brother time, and quite frankly, I really needed to put my feet up. I'd literally walked all over the city and was feeling every one of my forty-four years.

I got through a swarm of emails and replied to the urgent ones. Then I emailed Donella, my lead draftsperson, and roped her into taking on the critical jobs for tomorrow. She was more than capable of stepping up for a day because I was spending the day with Max.

And the truth was, I wasn't loving my job.

It was the first time ever that I'd not loved my job. I still loved architecture—that would never change—but I wasn't loving my *job*. This bullshit with Robert had put a cloud over everything to do with Brackett and Golding.

I didn't know what he was playing at, or what he was after. But I had bigger things to worry about.

I had to spend another day trying to up the ante in the cool stakes tomorrow with a seventeen-year-old punk kid, then spend the weekend with Cooper's parents.

My apartment, which had been just mine for four years and now was Cooper's home as well, was going to be very crowded for the weekend. With people who didn't particularly like me.

And the weird thing was? I was looking forward to it.

It meant a lot to Cooper, and I wanted it to work out for him. I wanted his parents to like me, to like *us*. Not for my sake, but for Cooper's.

I just hoped once they saw us, together, in our home, that they'd see the real us. That we were just a normal couple. Age differences aside, we *were* just a normal couple.

I had a quick shower to wash the grime of the city off me and crawled into bed. Not too long after, Cooper slid in behind me and wrapped his arm around my waist. He kissed the back of my head. "You impressed Max today."

"He had fun."

Cooper wriggled closer and nuzzled my neck. "What you did today... it means a lot to me."

I rolled over to face him and he hitched his leg over mine. His hand cupped my cheek and he kissed me. "I really do love you, Tom."

"I know," I whispered. "And I really love you."

He smiled and closed his eyes as if he were basking in sunshine. "I wish I could spend tomorrow with you and Max."

"I wish you could too," I said. "But I don't think I'll be earning any cool points with Max tomorrow. We have a very important dinner party we need to get produce for."

"You're taking him grocery shopping?"

"Yep."

"Yeah, you can hand your cool-card in," Cooper said with a smile.

"I have in-laws to impress, remember?"

"In-laws?"

"Well, your parents."

"In-laws?"

"Wrong word choice, again, huh?"

"Hmm," Cooper hummed. "On a scale of one to ten on the romantic marriage proposals, that was about a minus eighty."

"I didn't ask you!"

"You called my parents in-laws."

I chuckled and pecked his lips. "One of these days, I might ask you for real, and you'll shoot me down and break my heart."

"You have been asking me for real," he said, shaking his head. "I'll only say yes when you get it right."

"You're impossible."

"Ah, Tom, that's not getting it right. Were you *even* trying?"

"I wasn't even asking."

Cooper sighed. "You're impossible."

"I learned from the best."

Even in the dark, I could make out his grin. He kissed me with smiling lips, but then he stifled a yawn. "I know this is a first," he said, "but I'm too tired to do anything tonight."

"Oh, thank God," I said with a laugh. "I wasn't kidding about having to walk five hundred miles today."

"Aw, my poor baby," Cooper said in a baby's voice. "Did dat bad teenager wear you out today?"

I dug my fingers into his ribs, tickling him and making him squirm. "Yes, he did. He's almost as bad as you."

Cooper laughed. "I don't make you walk from one end of the city to the other."

"No, you wear me out in other ways."

"Better ways?"

"Much better ways."

Cooper pecked my lips with his. "Good." Then he rolled over and wiggled back against me. "I need big-spoon cuddles."

I laughed into the back of his head, but I nuzzled my nose into his hair, and put my arm around him. "I'll always be your big spoon."

He snorted. "Unless I'm being the big spoon. Then you'll be my little spoon."

"Always."

"Mmm, cute. But no marriage proposal should ever involve spoons."

I sighed. "Goodnight, Cooper."

I'D FORGOTTEN how teenagers could sleep. Max stumbled out of bed around ten, and according to him, even that was getting up early. The good part was, it gave me plenty of time to read emails, make phone calls, and basically work from home for a few hours.

Max griped about having to go grocery shopping, but once I explained it meant a lot to Cooper, he was okay with it. "He wants everything to be perfect for the dinner party tomorrow night," I said. "It's kind of a test by your parents of sorts, whether intentional or not, that Cooper and I are serious."

Max nodded, and only after a long stretch of silence did he reply. "They're trying to make an effort, you know."

"Your parents?"

"Yeah," he said. "They didn't like it at first, as you know.

But what you said to them about pushing Cooper away kinda hit home. Well, for Mom anyway."

"What do you mean?"

Max looked around the fresh produce store and shrugged. "Mom told Dad she'd intentionally lose her husband before she'd ever intentionally lose a child, and she warned him not to make her choose." Max picked up a durian and studied it like it was from outer space. "I don't think Dad would ever let it get to that. He loves Cooper, and what Coop said was right. If they didn't care if he liked boys or girls, then they shouldn't care how old they are." He held up the spiky fruit. "What the hell is this?"

"It's a durian," I said. "And I think your parents just want him to be happy."

"He is."

"I know."

"What do you do with it?"

"Pardon?"

"A durian. What do you do with it?"

"It's a fruit. And I have no clue. Apparently they're banned in some places in Asia because of the putrid smell. Why anyone would actually taste something that smelled like skunk, I'll never know."

Max dropped the fruit and wiped his hands on his pants. "Eww. That's just nasty."

I smiled. "I think your parents just need time."

"They miss Cooper."

"He moved to New York before we were together. He'd still be living away from home if he was with me or not."

"I know that. They know that," Max said. "But they still miss him."

"They've still got you at home," I said, as though it lessened the loss.

"Until next year, then I'll be going too." Max shrugged and spoke as though he couldn't have cared less. "I think Mom always hoped he'd come back to Chicago... But then he met you, and I think she knows he's not going anywhere in a hurry. I think that's what scared her the most, you know."

"I'm not holding him ransom here or anything," I said.

Max rolled his eyes. "I heard them talking one night, not long after you and Cooper visited. It's not really about you. It's about Cooper moving away and settling down. They weren't expecting him to bring anyone home, let alone you."

"Let alone me?"

"Yeah, you're like twice his age."

"Thanks for reminding me," I said. I was going to ask him if it bothered him, but I suddenly didn't want to know. Instead, I said, "Thanks for being honest with me."

Max shrugged again. "No worries. You know, growing up we were never that close. There's five years between us, so we were always at different schools, at different stages. Know what I mean?" he asked. "It's only now that he moved away that we're kind of getting along better. We make the effort to talk more, I guess."

"Cooper was so excited that you were coming."

"I came a day early to spend some time with him," he said quietly. "I didn't let him know I was coming in case he said no."

"He'd never say no, Max," I said softly. "He wishes he could have taken today off work to spend with you."

"Yeah, he said that. It was good to catch up with him last night," Max said with a bit of a smile. "He's real busy with work, isn't he?"

"He is," I agreed. "But you're more than welcome to come and stay anytime."

Max gave me a half-smile. "Don't tell him I didn't call him on purpose. He'll be mad."

I grinned at him. "Deal."

My cell phone rang, and when I pulled it from my pocket, Cooper's name flashed on the screen. I handed the phone to Max. "Here. You talk to him." I turned and looked over the rows of fruit to find what I was after.

"Hey," he said into the phone. "No, we're in the grocers. Tom's picking mangoes..." There was a moment's silence, then he said, "No, that's not a euphemism for anything. He's honestly looking at mangoes."

I laughed, but let him talk to Cooper while I picked all the fresh produce on Cooper's list. As I got to the register, Max handed me back my phone. "He needs to tell you something."

I took the phone. "Hey."

"I'm so fucking jealous of you two right now."

"Oh, sweetheart. I'm sorry."

"No, don't be," he said. "I just wish I was there, that's all. Max said he's had a pretty good day."

"Not as cool as yesterday."

"Well, no. But that would take some beating. What I was calling for, it looks like we're going to wrap up the Baurhenn job today. It's all but done. Louisa just needs to go over the job file and sign off on it."

"Oh, that's excellent!" I said into the phone. I handed my credit card to the cashier and paid for the groceries.

"I think they're having celebratory drinks somewhere," he said. "I should be there for that, but my parents and Max..."

"Tell them to have a little party at the office," I suggested. "That way your parents get to see where you work, and Max can go. If it's at a bar, then he can't, and, Cooper," I said, "he wants to spend time with you."

"I know," he said with a groan. "I'll see what I can organize, and let you know. Are you still able to collect my parents from the airport?"

I looked at my watch. I had three hours. "Of course I am."

"Tom, thank you."

"You can pay me back later."

"Dude!" Max said beside me, obviously hearing what I'd said to his brother. "Ew."

I laughed into the phone. "Cooper, I'll talk to you later."

We got home, I put everything away and checked emails, while Max spent the next two hours glued to his phone. His interest in doing anything was kind of wavering, but then I said we were heading to the airport, and he saw my Mercedes R171.

"Holy shit, dude!" he cried. "You serious?"

I laughed. "Cooper loves this car."

"I can see freakin' why!" he crowed. "Can I drive it?"

"No freakin' way," I copied his tone.

Max grinned all the way to the airport. Whether or not he knew I was nervous and needed some reinforcements, just like Cooper, he took charge. He chatted and kept me busy the whole time. His parents came through the terminal gates, searching the crowd. I think they were looking for Cooper, but they spotted Max and both of them smiled.

Then they saw me.

Andrew, Cooper's father, tried to smile but failed. However, Paula, Cooper's mother, managed just fine. It was a brief but polite hello, and the attention revolved around Max, which was fine with me.

Max told them all about the shirts he'd bought yesterday, for himself and Cooper, and the music he'd gotten. But then we got back to my car, and he started talking about it.

He assumed he'd be sitting in the front again, but I threw my thumb toward the back seat. Max grumbled at me, but he did climb through to the back. I'd never had anyone in the back seat of my car, so Max and Paula were the first. Which left Andrew in the front with me.

And funnily enough, he spoke to me. It was about the car, but it was unprompted conversation. Admittedly, I didn't know a great deal about cars in general, but I knew enough about this car to have a conversation with Cooper's father.

"Where is Cooper?" Paula asked from the back.

"At work," I said. "He's wrapping up his first project. It should be signed off on this afternoon. Well, he's hoping it will be. The developer is driving him insane." Then I said, "Actually, he won't be home till late, so he's hoping we can all go to his office. They might be having a little party to celebrate the completion of his first solo job. It's, um... it's kind of a big deal."

"Oh, okay," Paula said, unsure.

"But he's going to call to let us know," I told them. "It's just unfortunate timing that this particular job is being signed off on the same weekend of your visit. But that means he's free for the rest of the weekend. I think that's what he was aiming for. He's looking forward to having you all here."

In the rearview mirror, I watched as Paula smiled, then frowned as she must have remembered something. "Oh. Cooper presumed he'd have some work to catch up on tomorrow, and he told me not to get extra tickets to the show."

Max snorted. "He told you that because musicals suck."

"Max," Andrew chastised his son. "I'm sure Cooper would go and suffer along with the rest of us for the sake of his mother."

Max nodded in agreement, and Paula rolled her eyes. I couldn't help but laugh. Not that what Andrew had said wasn't funny, just that I'd never expected Cooper's sense of humor to come from his dad.

"Well, Cooper has a dinner planned for you tomorrow night," I told them. "So while you're out at the show, it will give us time to get it all ready."

We got to the apartment, and I showed them to the spare room. "I had housecleaning change the linen today," I told them. "Max, you're on the sofa."

"Oh, nice," he said. "Kick me out." Then after a second, he cocked his head. "You have a housekeeper? So I didn't need to make my bed this morning?"

I didn't get a chance to reply. Paula beat me to it. She hissed at him. "Max. Don't be rude."

Max rolled his eyes. "Don't stress. Tom's cool."

I don't know why it embarrassed me, but his acknowledgment made me blush. "Ah, bathroom through that door," I said, pointing the way. "That's mine and Cooper's room," I added, then regretted literally pointing to the bedroom I shared with their son. I cleared my throat and led them back out to the living room. "Balcony out there."

It was obvious they were a little impressed by the apartment—the place Cooper now called home. But it was still a bit awkward.

Thankfully Cooper called soon after and, after chatting for a short while, invited us all to his office for some celebratory drinks. Paula and Andrew suggested they take a walk for a look at the city before we were due to leave, so the three of them left for an hour or so. And quite frankly, it was a much-needed reprieve.

The first meeting with his parents—on my own, no less—had gone quite well, I thought.

I called the office and spoke to Jennifer for a while. She said nothing was that urgent that couldn't wait until Monday, that Robert was curious as to my absence, but apart from that, all was well.

I spent the rest of my time alone choosing something to wear that wasn't too old or too young, wishing Cooper was there to just pick it for me. So I phoned him, and he roared with laughter. "Just pick something," he said. "Be yourself. They will love you."

"Cooper," I whined, rather childishly.

"Your black jeans, white button-down shirt, and my charcoal vest," he rattled off quickly.

"Okay."

"God, Tom, are you that easy?"

I sighed. "You know I am." I clicked off the call before he could answer.

But an hour later, dressed in the outfit he had suggested and with his family in tow, I walked through the lobby of Arlington for the second time in as many days. The receptionist nodded me through this time, and we walked down the hall to the large communal office room where the party was being held.

I was quite looking forward to it.

Until I saw Xavier Baurhenn with his arm around Cooper.

Fuck.

CHAPTER NINE

COOPER SAW us as we walked in, and peeled himself away from under Xavier's grasp as we approached. He hugged his parents first, bumped fists with his brother, then slid his arm around my waist. "Thank you," he whispered, leaning into me.

"Is he annoying you?" I didn't have to say Xavier's name.

"Hasn't stopped yet," he said, then turned to his parents, who were watching us. "Let me show you around."

Cooper took his parents and showed them around his office, the place where he spent so much time, and in particular the boards and scaled model of the project he'd just completed.

Which left me alone with Xavier. Thankfully before we could say more than a brief hello, Louisa saved me. "Tom!" she said, kissing me on the cheek. "So good to see you again."

"Louisa," I said. "Exciting times for Cooper."

"Oh my God," she said. "He deserves this. He's really

worked hard for this." Then she included Xavier. "Xavier can attest to that. He's gone above and beyond."

The slimy bastard smiled at me. "Oh, he sure has," he said with innuendo dripping off every word. "Mr. Elkin," he said, sipping his champagne, "it's good to see you again. But if you'll excuse me, I'll be with the man of the hour." He looked over toward Cooper, then back at me as if daring me.

Xavier turned on his heel and walked over toward Cooper and his family, and Louisa handed me a glass of champagne. She put her glass to her mouth and mumbled, "He's an arrogant prick."

I hid my smile behind my drink. "Cooper can't stand him."

"Oh, I know," Louisa said, still smiling behind her glass of champagne.

We watched as Xavier introduced himself to Cooper's parents and brother.

"I think the reason Cooper pushed so hard to finish the job was to be rid of him. It's a blessing and a curse that Cooper had a Baurhenn job as his first," Louisa said. "Great on the portfolio, but putting up with Xavier is..." She seemed stuck for the right word.

"Trying?"

"I was going to say 'skin-crawling.'"

I laughed. "Well, there's that."

We were interrupted by two people whom I'd met before. Skye and Tyson were happy for Cooper, and as much as they assured me it was his job and his alone, Cooper would assure me it was a team effort.

It was pretty obvious word had spread around the office that the 'Tom' Cooper had talked about was, in fact, Thomas Elkin. There wasn't a huge number of people there, but they all eyed me and took turns at introducing themselves.

I kept a bit of an eye on Cooper as he mingled, and over the course of the evening, I saw first-hand just how much Xavier touched him. No wonder Cooper hated to be around him. And it seemed the more glasses of champagne Xavier had, the sleazier he got. Admittedly, it wasn't just with Cooper, it was with anyone, but it still irked me.

I finally had a quiet moment, so I grabbed a glass of champagne for me and a soda for Max and saved him from dying of absolute boredom. "What's with the douche-king?" Max asked, giving a pointed nod to Xavier.

I laughed again. God, he was so like his brother. "He's the grandson of a property-developer millionaire who's been given permission from his father to try his hand at real estate development."

Max sipped his soda. "He's a dick."

I snorted into my drink just as Cooper snuck up beside me and slipped his arm around my waist. "Oh my God," he said. "This is a bit insane. I've just been lined up to do an interview for *Architect* magazine next month. Can you believe that?"

"I can," I said.

"We were just talking about the douchebag," Max said with another pointed glance at Xavier, who was talking rather loudly to a group of Cooper's coworkers.

Cooper gritted his teeth. "Thank God today's the last day. After tonight, I'm done with him." Then Cooper looked at me. "You don't seem to mind letting him put his grubby hands on me."

"Mind?" I asked. "It's disgusting."

"Well, tell him to stop it," Cooper said with a smile, like it was the most obvious thing to do.

I spoke to him through smiling lips and gritted teeth. "I didn't want to make a scene in front of your colleagues."

Cooper rolled his eyes, which silently said, *That's the lamest excuse ever.*

"After tonight, you don't have to see him again," I said, trying to placate him, just as Paula and Andrew came up to us.

"It's getting kind of late," Paula said, obviously wanting to go home. "It's been a long day."

But then, like the slimeball he was, Xavier came over to us and put his arm around Cooper's shoulders. "How about," he said just to him, "we go out? This party is all but over, but the night is still young."

Cooper's eyes darted to mine, so I stepped in closer to Xavier, looked pointedly at his offending arm around Cooper. "The funny thing about architecture, Xavier, is that there's a distinct rule on space. You don't encroach on what's not yours," I said, still smiling but with fair warning in my tone. "There are boundaries. You should learn them."

Xavier shrugged like he didn't care, like the arrogant little fuck he was. "My school days are over. No one owns me," he said, which I'm sure was a jab at Cooper. "I'm free to do what I want."

"I'll be sure to tell your father all about that," I told him cheerfully. "I'm meeting with him on Wednesday. We're discussing tenders for the Eccleston Apartment complex. I'm sure he'll be very interested to hear it."

A few shades paler, Xavier smiled, though it was more of a sneer. "Well, then," he said. "I should be going. Pleasure to meet you all," he said to Cooper's parents. Then he turned to Cooper but glanced at me first. He extended his hand, which Cooper shook. "It's been a pleasure. Hope we can continue this professional relationship in the future with new projects."

It was a practiced spiel, translucent as he was.

When Xavier had gone, Cooper shuddered. "Are you really meeting the Baurhenn group on Wednesday?"

"No," I said with a smile. "But he doesn't know that."

Max laughed. "He was whistling a different tune after that, though."

Cooper chuckled but looked at his parents. "Come on, let's go home."

We said goodbye to Louisa and the others, and when we stepped into the elevator, Paula sighed and said, "It just goes to show that all the money in the world can't buy you class. That guy was a..."

Max finished for her, "A douche!"

Cooper smiled and leaned into me. "Yeah, the last few weeks have been... character-building."

Cooper's father looked at his son and said, "Don't know how you haven't punched him."

Then Paula looked at me and said, "I don't know how *you* haven't punched him!"

I laughed quietly. "If it wouldn't have ended Cooper's career, I probably would have."

Cooper snorted and shook his head at me, disbelievingly. "No, you wouldn't have. You'd find some other way to shame him, professionally, publicly, by proving what a dick he is. But not punching him."

I conceded with a nod. "Maybe."

"The likes of Xavier Baurhenn will never amount to anything," Cooper said confidently. "Not long term. I don't care who his parents are, he has no integrity."

I smiled at him and kissed the side of the head, not caring if his parents were right there, just as the elevator doors opened. As we walked through the lobby, Cooper took my hand and asked, "Have you guys had enough to eat? We could pick up a pizza if you want?"

And so began the friendly debate over New York pizza versus Chicago pizza, which lasted until the last slice was eaten and I bade Cooper and his family goodnight. I thought they could use some time to catch up. Cooper had missed them, and even though it was late, they sat around the living room talking long after I went to bed.

I WOKE up to the sound of banging on my door. I sat bolt upright, making Cooper, who had been half wrapped around me, startle awake. "Wuh?"

"Cooper, get your ass out of bed and make me pancakes!"

I sagged.

Max.

Cooper laughed sleepily and fell back on the bed with a groan. If Max was awake, it meant his parents were, and figuring I'd rather not venture out in front of them half-naked in my sleepwear, I headed straight for the shower.

When I came out, appropriately dressed in jeans and a T-shirt, there was a wonderful smell of bacon and pancakes cooking, and Max and Cooper were arguing.

"Dude," Max said, "you need to add the bacon to the batter."

"No, you don't," Cooper argued. "You fry the bacon first, then add the batter."

"Mom!" Max called out. "Please tell him he's doing it wrong."

I walked in behind the kitchen counter and headed straight for the coffee machine. Cooper smiled at me and said, "Tom, tell him how it's done."

"Well, I would say fry the bacon first."

Cooper grinned hugely at me, and Max groaned. "You *have* to say that. Mom!" Max called again. "They're picking on me!"

Cooper launched himself at his brother, collecting him in a headlock and dragging him out through the living room to the verandah, where I presumed their parents were sitting enjoying the morning sun. But just as they got to the door, Paula walked through it. She looked at her two sons and sighed. "Cooper, leave your brother alone." It sounded like it was something she'd said a thousand times.

Max spoke from the headlock he was still in. "Mom, do you cook bacon first or in the pancake batter?"

Cooper looked at his mom and smiled, as though having his brother in a headlock was nothing out of the ordinary. "Tell him I'm right."

"I always cook the bacon first," she said.

Cooper raised his free arm and crowed in victory. But then Andrew called out, "I pour the batter over the bacon."

Cooper dropped his arm, deflated, and Max sprang up and out of his headlock. "Ha! Told ya!"

Before Max barely had the words out, Cooper tackled him onto the sofa. Paula looked at me. I smiled, shrugged, and turned the bacon. "Can I get you a refill?" I asked her, nodding to her coffee cup.

She smiled and walked over to the kitchen island. "I can get it," she said. After she'd poured herself another, she leaned against the kitchen counter, holding the cup with her two hands. "Boys!" she chided. "Stop wrestling."

Cooper got off his brother, ruffled his hair for good

measure, then walked into the kitchen. He took the tongs out of my hands, snapped them at me, then ordered Max to set the table.

"I was quite capable of turning bacon," I said.

He grinned at me and bumped his hip into mine. "I have it all under control," he said. "You just need to stand there, drinking coffee and looking handsome."

I rolled my eyes at him, and Paula smiled behind her coffee cup. And the rest of breakfast went pretty much the same. We all sat around the dining table and listened as Cooper told stories of his time here in New York.

He was so excited and happy to have his family here, and I couldn't help but smile at him as he chatted animatedly. And as they all got dressed and ready for their lunch and theater show, Cooper and I cleaned up the mess in the kitchen. Yes, it was cute to watch them wrestle and jibe at each other, but tidy cooks they weren't. And as his parents and brother were getting ready, walking in and out of the open living area, every chance he got, Cooper would grope my ass or kiss me.

We finally got the mess cleaned up, and they all looked very well-dressed and ready to go. Paula offered one last chance for us to go with them. "Can't, Mom," Cooper told her. "I have the best dinner to cook. It's gonna take a while. By the time you get back, it'll all be done and we can sit down and you'll tell us all about the show."

Paula looked at me. "Are you really sure?"

"It's fine, truly," I told her.

"How come they have a choice?" Andrew asked. "I don't mind staying and cooking, if it means I get out of going to this musical."

Max gasped at his father. "You'd leave me to go alone? Nice. Real nice."

"You're both going," Paula said, putting an end to that conversation.

Cooper laughed and offered to walk them down to the lobby. "I want you to meet Lionel," he said. "Then I need to come back up here and cook up a storm."

When he was done harassing poor Lionel, he walked back into the apartment. I was in the kitchen with most of the ingredients on the counter. "Okay, what do we need to do first?" I asked. "I thought we might start—"

Cooper spun me around and pressed me against the kitchen counter. "We need to fuck."

My mouth fell open. "Such a romantic way to put it."

He took my hand and led me to our bedroom. "There won't be anything romantic about it," he mumbled. "I can't wait any longer. I thought they'd never leave."

I laughed, but then he turned and kissed me, hard. He was so damn eager. And hard.

I kissed him back, running my fingers through his hair while he slipped his tongue into my mouth. He walked us backwards to the bed, but before I could push him onto it, he turned in my arms and leaned over the mattress. Quickly undoing the button on his cargos, he slid them over his hips, exposing his bare ass to me.

"Cooper," I whispered gruffly.

"Just do it, Tom," he said. "I really need you."

I reached over to the bedside table and pulled out one foil packet and the small bottle of lubricant. I undid my jeans and pulled my dick from my briefs, tore open the condom wrapper, and rolled the latex barrier down my cock.

Only then did I notice Cooper, rubbing his slicked fingers over his ass, inside his hole.

"Fuck."

Cooper moaned. "Please. Tom, I'm ready. I just need you."

I rubbed some lube over my cock, and with my jeans still around my ass and Cooper's cargos down to his thighs, I pressed against him. As the head of my cock breached his hole, Cooper gripped the bedspread and moaned. And the further I slid into him, the louder he became.

I leaned over him. "You okay?"

"Don't stop," he bit out. Then he groaned again. "Fuck, Tom."

Putting my hands on the bed above his shoulders, I leaned over him and kissed the back of his neck, and I rolled my hips into him, over and over. Cooper gripped my hands and my wrists and he lifted his ass for me. It didn't take long for that familiar draw in my belly, in my balls, and I knew I was close to coming.

Then Cooper bucked his hips, like he was working my cock, and my body seized and my senses obliterated as I filled the condom. Cooper moaned deep and low as I came, and when I pulled out of him, I spun him around and leaned him back onto the bed.

I lifted his legs so his feet were on the edge of the bed and took his still-hard dick into my mouth. I slid two fingers into his ass, twisting them up, searching, feeling for his gland.

His reaction told me I'd found it.

He gripped the bedspread in his fists and he threw his head back. "Fuck!" he growled out. "There!"

I sucked him and fucked him with my fingers, and when his cock pulsed in my mouth, he shot come down my throat. I pulled my fingers out of him, my mouth off him, licking as I went and he squirmed under my touch. I leaned over him and put my head on his chest.

His heart was hammering and he clumsily put his hand on my hair. "Fuck," he murmured. "That was exactly what I needed."

I looked up at him and smiled. "What we need now is a shower."

Cooper squirmed again. "No round two?"

I grinned at him. "We have dinner to make."

"We can order takeout."

I barked out a laugh and, taking his hand, pulled him off the bed. "No, we can't. You've been planning this for a week."

He followed me into the bathroom and as I threw the used condom in the trash, he slapped my ass. "I hate it when you're responsible."

"I love it when you're horny," I said. I turned the taps on in the shower and pointed to the water. "Now get in. I'll make sure you're all clean."

He stepped up close to me. "You'd better be thorough."

I pecked his lips. "Just do as you're told, Jones."

He raised an eyebrow at me. "Bossy in the bedroom, I'll take any day. Bossy out of the bedroom, not so much."

I laughed. "You're the bossiest person I know."

"And you love it," he replied, stepping in under the streams of water.

"Is there any point in me arguing that?" I asked, stepping in behind him.

His answer was short and sweet. "Not if you're smart."

I pressed him up against the tiles and scraped my teeth against the back of his neck. "Oh, I'm smart," I murmured.

He moaned and his skin covered with goosebumps, even under the hot water. "If you do that again, Tom, we'll be ordering in dinner."

I smiled into the skin on his shoulder but picked up the

bar of soap and started lathering his body. I soaped him over, feeling every inch of his skin under my hands, and he soon turned around so he could kiss me.

We made out like college kids in the shower, and still even had everything done for dinner by the time his family came back.

And yes, Paula told us about the musical they'd just seen, while Andrew and Max rolled their eyes. I poured some wine, and as we served dinner, talk turned to the food, and I promised them that I was just the apprentice—Cooper was the one who did everything. I just did as I was told.

"Tom very rarely does what he's told," Cooper said, taking a bite of his chicken.

"Which is rather surprising, considering how bossy he is," I replied to everyone at the table.

Paula laughed at that. But then Cooper said, "Tom asked me to marry him."

I dropped my fork. "I what?"

Despite the stunned silence at the table, Cooper rolled his eyes. "You know you have."

I looked at his parents. "I haven't, not really."

"Well, okay," Cooper added, "so they weren't traditional proposals by any means."

His mother's eyes were wide. "They? As in a few?"

"Well, I keep saying no," Cooper told her, as if he were talking about the wine.

"I haven't asked him," I told everyone again. "He keeps telling me I have, but I've said no such thing." I didn't dare look at Andrew. He'd only just started to warm to me. I pushed my plate away and decided that drinking wine was a much better idea.

Max burst out laughing. "And that, boys and girls, is what we call a conversation stopper."

Cooper laughed, and, more surprisingly, Andrew did too. "Good one, Grandpa," Andrew said, which confused me even more. I was, however, one hundred percent certain I would never understand the Joneses' sense of humor.

Then Cooper said, "Okay, so he hasn't technically. I just thought I'd do a Grandpa. You know, keep the tradition alive."

According to legend, Cooper's grandfather, at a family gathering once, had stood up and announced he'd won a few million dollars, which he hadn't. He'd just wanted to spark up conversation, see people's reactions purely for entertainment purposes. And now, apparently, at most Jones family functions someone made some outlandish comment, just for laughs.

"I'm guessing the sense of humor is hereditary," I said, still preferring my wine.

"Well, my father was a very funny man," Andrew said. And so the conversation resumed around the table. I did notice Paula looking at Cooper a little weirdly, though he seemed oblivious, as they talked about some cousin I'd never heard of.

Later that night, when Cooper was sound asleep beside me, and unable to sleep myself, I got up for a drink of water. Knowing Max was asleep on the sofa, I didn't turn on any lights, and after I'd poured myself a glass of water, I noticed the door to the balcony was open.

Thinking someone might have left it open, I stuck my head out to make sure I wasn't locking anyone out, when I found Paula looking out over the city. I must have startled her, because she put her hand to her heart. "Jesus."

"Sorry," I said softly, grateful I'd worn sleep pants *and* a shirt to bed. "I was just checking I didn't lock anyone out here or if the door was just left open." Then I added, "I was just getting a drink."

"I was just enjoying the view," she said with a smile. "It's so quiet up here."

Not sure if I should but not wanting her to think I was ignoring her, I walked out and leaned against the balcony railing, overlooking the city. "It's really beautiful."

She smiled and sighed, and for a long moment we both just stood there and admired the city lights. Paula had been a little quiet since Cooper's marriage statement at dinner. "I'm sorry about what Cooper said about us getting married," I offered quietly. "I haven't asked him. Not officially. But he keeps alluding to the fact as though I have." Paula didn't answer me, so I added, "I just didn't want you to think I was misleading you or that we were hiding anything, because we're not." She still didn't say anything, so I thought I'd aim for funny. "He keeps telling me I'm proposing but then turns me down, so I can't win anyway."

Paula looked at me then, and smiled. But she still never said anything, and I realized I'd probably said too much.

"Well, I'll leave you to it," I said, taking a step toward the door. "Goodnight."

Before I walked back inside, she said, "He used to do that, as a kid."

I stopped and looked at her, waiting for her to continue.

Paula looked back out to the city but said, "When he was younger, he used to do the same thing. He'd twist the story all around, as though buying him a new bike was my idea, then tell me I didn't have to. Or the time for his birthday, he wanted a new phone or a new laptop, he'd bring it up in conversation. I'd say something about it and he'd tell me I was bad at keeping secrets about what I was getting him."

I chuckled quietly. "That sounds like him."

Then her smiled died. "It's hard for me to watch him grow up. No matter how accomplished he is or how successful he is, he's still my little boy."

"He'll always be your son," I told her honestly. "He loves you very much."

"He loves you too," she said, looking back out to the city before looking at me.

I held her gaze. "Yes, he does."

She gave me a sad smile. "He wants you to ask him to marry you."

I ran her words through my head a few times and still wasn't sure how she had come to that conclusion. "Pardon?"

"He wants you to ask him to marry you," she repeated. "That's why he keeps bringing it up. That's what he does. Whether it's a new bike, a new phone, a computer... that's what he does. He keeps talking about it like it's your idea."

I looked back out across the neon-lit sky so Paula wouldn't see the surprise on my face. But then she startled me by laughing. "He told me you bought him some Prada boots. Was it your idea or did he suggest them *as though* it was your idea."

I smiled. "It was his idea."

Paula smiled. "See? That's what he does." Then she looked back out over the New York skyline. "You don't seem too deterred by the idea."

"I'm not," I told her honestly. "But for what it's worth, he might think he's ready, but he's not."

Paula laughed again. "Oh, Tom. You know he always gets what he wants, right? Whether he works hard for it or simply demands it."

I couldn't help but chuckle. "I guess."

She nodded knowingly and sighed again, looking out

over the city. "For what it's worth, Tom, I'm not opposed to it either. I thought I would be, but I'm really not. I just want him happy, and I can see that he's happy with you."

I gave her a smile. "Thank you." I bade her goodnight, then slid into bed with Cooper. Even though he was sound asleep, I kissed the back of his head and smiled and my let my dreams take me.

CHAPTER TEN

WE SAID goodbye to Cooper's family at the airport, and he grinned the entire trip home and for most of the afternoon. He was still buzzed about having his family here and the acceptance they seemed to show in regards to our relationship.

I didn't tell Cooper about the conversation I'd had with his mother. Though I had to admit, I liked knowing. I liked knowing that this man wanted to marry me, even if he didn't know that I knew.

I pulled out my laptop and sat at the dining table when Cooper walked over and kissed the side of my head. "Whatcha doing?"

"I need to catch up on work," I explained. "I haven't been in the office for four days."

"Surely they can't be pissed at you for that," he said.

"I don't care if they are," I said honestly. "I've enjoyed this weekend, and I wouldn't change it."

"You were amazing this weekend."

I smiled up at him. "I missed a lot of family stuff

working so much. It's about time I spent time on what's really important."

"Well, work, then dinner, then you can do what's *really* important." Then he added, "You know I'm what's important, don't you? I meant that you can do me."

I laughed. "I got the reference, yes."

He leaned down and nuzzled my neck. "You know, if you haven't worked all weekend, another few hours won't hurt." He then rubbed my shoulders, massaging me with his fingers. "Leave it until tomorrow. We can lie on the sofa and watch some hockey or something. We've had the perfect weekend, don't ruin it now with work. Let the likes of Robert Chandler ruin your day tomorrow. Spend today with me."

WHEN I WALKED into my office on Monday morning, I wondered what would greet me. But Jennifer smiled, asked me all about my extended weekend and how I had coped with Cooper's parents. We chatted for a brief moment, she told me my coffee was on my desk, then it was business as usual.

But then at three o'clock, Jennifer knocked quietly and let herself into my office. "Robert wants to see us both," she said in a hushed tone.

"When?"

She looked at the clock on the wall. "Now."

Well, shit. I closed the file on my desk, then Jennifer and I walked the short distance to Robert's office. His receptionist buzzed us through, but before we got to the door, I stopped us. "Jennifer, whatever he says, it doesn't matter. It will all be okay."

And with that, we walked inside.

Robert sat smugly at his desk, and Peter Sleiman and Donald Croft sat at the side of the desk. As surprised as I was to see them, I gave them a smile and said, "Good afternoon," as Jennifer and I both sat down across from Robert.

They both nodded, but it was Robert who spoke.

"I have asked Peter and Donald to sit in on this meeting because I believe some interesting developments have come to light."

He then licked his fingers, like the uncouth slob he was, and turned the first page of the file in front of him. I recognized it immediately. It was Cooper's approval for the Baurhenn job.

I looked at Robert curiously. "How are those plans relevant to anything here?"

Robert smiled at me but then looked at Jennifer. "Jennifer, I need to remind you that you're here in an official capacity, and what you say will be taken seriously." He looked back down to the file in front of him. "Did you request the job files from archives for the 1994 Graham's Corporation job Mr. Elkin did here in Riverdale District?"

"I retrieve a lot of files for Mr. Elkin," Jennifer told him.

Robert stared at her. "These Brackett and Golding plans were used by Mr. Elkin for personal reasons. He shared these plans and specifications with a Mr. Cooper Jones, who then went on to win the contract to build for the Baurhenn Group. I wouldn't have known this, only the plans that Mr. Jones submitted for approval have a distinctively similar façade—elements that have Tom Elkin written all over them."

"I wouldn't remember specific files," Jennifer said. "Though if you have archives records of the request, then you already know."

He smiled again. "Yes, you're quite right."

I sighed. "Those plans are available at the City Library. Hell, they're probably online. You'd only have to drive down the damn street to see the façade, Robert. Any architect knows the city has design clauses and restrictions because it's pre-1940 with the Preservation Committee, and anyone with half a brain would know that what was approved by city planners less than ten years ago would be approved again." I shook my head at him. "You're really clutching at straws this time, Robert."

Robert ignored me completely and again turned to Jennifer. "Jennifer, were you aware that Brackett and Golding also filed submissions for the Baurhenn job? And that, in fact, helping another firm win a contract is a breach of policy?"

"Oh, enough, Robert," I said flatly. "For fuck's sake, that's enough. If you have something against me, if you're that damn homophobic, you speak to me, not Jennifer."

"Tom, it's fine," Jennifer started to say.

"No, it's not," I answered. "It's far from fine. He wants to get rid of me and is using you as bait, and that's *far from fine*."

Robert was still smiling, as though it was just the reaction he was after. "Tom, it's also been brought to our attention that you may have used the Brackett and Golding contracts you've completed to purchase real estate in districts you knew were undergoing development."

I think my mouth fell open. "You can't be serious. You taught me how to do that, Robert, remember? When I worked with you when I first started here, you told me it was a smart financial decision to follow developmental trends."

"No, I never," he lied outright. Then he changed the subject again, swiftly putting the emphasis back on me. "And then there's the little problem of you... and your intern."

"Oh, that's enough, Robert. Enough." I shook my head. "I'm not even going to justify that with an answer. The problem here is that I'm gay, but, of course, you can't say that trying to fire me, can you?"

"The problem is with your work ethic and bringing this company into disrepute."

I laughed at that. "I'm done." I stood up. "I'm so fucking done here."

Jennifer stood up beside me. "You're what?"

"I'm done. I quit. Hereby tender my resignation, citing Robert as a homophobic asshole, and I'm better off some-where else that doesn't confine creativity and expressionism."

Jennifer shook her head. She didn't say anything, but she looked worried, scared even.

I put my hand on her arm. "I know you don't want to work for anyone else. But this way you don't have to. You can come work for me."

Then I turned back to the other two men seated at the table. "I've done nothing wrong, but I won't stand for this. You can have my termination papers drawn up and forwarded to my lawyer."

Jennifer stood beside me and looked to the other men sitting with Robert. "Gentlemen, Robert's already familiar with Tom's legal firm, he can give you those details. In case he's forgotten, it's the same lawyers who took care of a little problem for Robert about fifteen years ago when he got his intern pregnant. You remember that, don't you, Robert?"

Robert's face went red, his eyes bugged out, and he sputtered something unintelligible. I couldn't stop the bubble of laughter that escaped me. This was news to me.

Jennifer folded her arms. "Did you forget I've been here as long as you, Robert? I've seen every single thing that's gone on in this office for the past sixteen years, including your indiscretions with numerous young female staff. More recently, how you've snooped for information on Tom, trying to ruin his career for your own satisfaction, how you've intimidated staff to try to leach details. I've seen it all, and you'll do well to remember that." Jennifer sniffed, then raised her chin and spoke to Peter and Donald. "I'll be happy to testify to anything I've just said. But you can finalize my papers and entitlements and forward them with Tom's papers to his lawyer."

I looked back at Robert, who was now looking a little pale. I would have smiled at him if he wasn't so pitiful. Instead, I said, "You, Robert, are a disgrace to this firm." And with that, Jennifer and I walked out of his office. We packed up our belongings, to a hushed disbelief across the entire office floor.

And with a strangely enlightened feeling, we walked out of Brackett and Golding for the last time.

I HEARD the familiar sound of keys at the front door, and I laughed. "Cooper's home," I said, and Jennifer started to giggle.

Cooper walked in and stopped when he saw Jennifer was in our living room, sitting with me on the sofa. We were both grinning like idiots so he smiled cautiously at us. Then he saw the two empty bottles of wine and the half-empty third and looked at me. "Celebrating something?"

"Kind of," I said, and Jennifer giggled again.

"We're unemployed," she added cheerfully.

Cooper dropped his messenger bag along with his jaw. "You're what?"

"I prefer the term 'newly self-employed,'" I amended.

Jennifer laughed again, and Cooper sat down next to me, ignoring our drunken merriment. "Tom, what the hell happened?" he asked. "Did something happen with Robert?"

"Well, yes," I said. "He called Jennifer and me in for a meeting with Peter and Donald and threw accusations at me. First, that I'd helped you secure the Baurhenn contract because it 'looked like my work.' Which I told him was bullshit. Then he accused me of profiting personally by using Brackett and Golding information to purchase real estate in areas about to be developed. Which is kind of true, but it's not illegal, and anyone with half a brain and the financial backing can do it. But then," I continued, "*then* he tried to blame Jennifer, and I drew the line."

"You quit?"

"Kind of. I was pushed," I said, taking another sip of wine. "I told them to forward my termination papers to my lawyers. Peter Sleiman didn't look too pleased with Robert. I'm guessing we haven't heard the last of it."

"Tom," Cooper whispered. He shook his head, unsure of what else to say. "I can't believe it."

"You know what?" I asked rhetorically. "This isn't what I had planned. At all. But I think this could be the best thing to happen to me..." Then I corrected, "Well, the second-best thing to happen to me." I took his hand. "You're the best thing to ever happen to me."

Cooper ignored what I'd said. "Tom..." He shook his head. "Oh, my God. I can't believe it."

Giving him a moment to get his head around it, I asked him if he wanted some wine. He shook his head. Instead he asked, "Why didn't you call me?"

"It only happened late this afternoon," I said. "Jennifer and I left and thought we could do with a drink. Here we are! I knew you wouldn't be far away, and I didn't want you to worry."

He rubbed his temples and forehead. "Was it because of me? Really? Because I—"

"No," I interrupted him. "No. It had nothing to do with you, Cooper, and everything to do with me. Not you, so don't even think that."

He shook his head again and exhaled through puffed cheeks. "And you two are celebrating? Or commiserating?"

"Celebrating," Jennifer and I answered at the same time, which made Jennifer start to laugh again.

"I told Tom last week I didn't want to work for anyone else at that firm," Jennifer explained. "I'm near retirement age anyway, but Tom said he'd need me if he's going to go out on his own."

Cooper's eyes shot to mine. "On your own?"

"Yes," I said, nodding. "I'm going to do my own thing. Someone taught me to say 'fuck it' every now and then and do what's in my heart."

Cooper's eyes then darted to Jennifer. "I apologize for the language, Jennifer." Then he swatted my arm. "Don't swear in front of a lady."

Jennifer roared laughing. "Oh, Cooper, you're a sweetheart. Thank you, but I must be going home. I've had far too much to drink to keep up appearances"—she smoothed down her hair—"and will bid both you lovely gentlemen goodnight."

"I'll walk you down and see you into a cab," Cooper said, not taking no for an answer.

I kissed Jennifer on the cheek, told her goodnight, and Cooper returned a few minutes later, and we played a game of 374 questions. He was shocked, but after he got over that initial reaction, he could see my point of view.

Yes, it was scary and daunting and exciting and new.

"I needed the challenge," I said. "I've seen what you do, all the new concepts and principles, and I want to be able to have the freedom to do that too."

And just like that, he understood.

"Have you eaten?" he asked.

"Have you?"

"No," he answered. "What do you feel like?"

I was going to answer something sex-related, but feeling the wine buzz in my system, I said, "Pizza," instead.

<hr>

THE NEXT DAY, just as Cooper was about to leave, the intercom buzzed. "Sorry to bother you, Mr. Elkin. Jennifer Huddleston is here to see you."

I slowly walked over to the intercom and pressed the button. "Does she have coffee?"

"Yes, sir, she does."

"Then please, let her up."

Cooper laughed. "Bit hungover, are you?"

"How much wine did I drink last night?"

"About a bottle too much."

"Do you have to talk so loud?" I asked. "Because honestly, I don't think that's necessary."

Cooper laughed again, just as there was a knock on the door. He let Jennifer in, who brought with her a tray of to-go coffee cups. She handed one to Cooper, which he took gratefully. "I wasn't sure if you'd still be here," she said.

"Just about to leave," he said. "How are you feeling this morning?"

"Oh, I'm fine," she answered.

She looked fine. I, on the other hand, felt like crap. "Could you two keep it down a bit, thanks," I mumbled from the kitchen.

I was trying to fill the coffee machine when Jennifer handed me a coffee. "I'm feeling every ounce of the wine we drank last night."

"I made him get up and shower, at least," Cooper gloated. Then he kissed my cheek. "You two seriously aren't going into Brackett and Golding today?"

I shook my head and sipped my life-saving coffee. "No."

"But we have much to do," Jennifer said. As she rattled off a list of things to do to a very amused Cooper, I sank back onto the sofa with my coffee and picked up my notepad.

"Can you two do all that important talking a little quieter?" I mumbled. "My head hurts."

Cooper laughed and walked over to kiss the top of my head. He wished Jennifer the best of luck and, with a grin, left for work.

"Tom," Jennifer called me by my first name, and it was nice to have her so relaxed with me. Gone was the stiff-backed personal assistant. She sat down across from me. "Hungover or not, I think we need—"

Yet, she was still my ever-efficient Jennifer. I interrupted her by handing her my notepad. "Business plan—financials, projections, goals, and mission statement," I said, taking a sip of my coffee. "Hungover, yes, but I'm still me."

Jennifer grinned. "Okay, so where do we start?"

CHAPTER ELEVEN

AS I DROVE out of the city, I thought about the last month. It had been interesting, that was for sure. It had been four weeks since I'd left Brackett and Golding. Four weeks of getting my own business started. It was only early days, but things were going well.

Peter Sleiman had called to tell me Robert had been fired. Jennifer's claims of numerous affairs with staff had proved true, and Peter said they really didn't like the way he'd tried to defame me. Robert had admitted to 'not appreciating working with a homosexual' and finding my relationship with Cooper a 'bad reflection of what Brackett and Golding stood for.'

They'd asked me to come back to work for them, and I, of course, had said no.

I loved working for myself. Along with the stress of starting over and fear of failure, there was also a freedom. A freedom of time, yes, but a freedom of expression. I'd been studying up on ecologically sustainable development and had a fantastic teacher in Cooper.

Cooper had been amazing. He'd work all day at Arlington, then come home and want to know everything I'd done. I only had two contracts in the first four weeks—though they were pretty big jobs. But he was fascinated with the inception of my business, getting more excited with each step I took.

He was almost as excited as me.

I was still working from home. I'd told Jennifer we'd look for an office soon, but while I started out, working from the apartment was logical, practical, and economical.

I insisted Jennifer start with six-hour days, for the same pay of course. The truth was, I couldn't have done it without her. She was more than a personal assistant. She was like some organizational guru who held it all together for me.

She argued about the hours, of course, but I explained that this was about reducing stress and getting back to basics. Not like starting over, but more like regrouping and doing what felt right, not what was expected. So if she wanted to take some hours to see her grandkids at school, then she absolutely should.

When I put it like that, she didn't argue. She was amazing and had helped me more than she could possibly know.

But it was Cooper...

In less than twelve months, he'd changed my life. He'd changed the way I thought, the way I saw the world.

He'd changed *me*.

I got out of my car, took a single key from my pocket, and opened the door. It was a small, cottage-style bungalow not too far from the Casa in the Hamptons. It wasn't on the beach, though, it was on a nature reserve.

It was a disaster.

Half-gutted, walls missing, drywall strewn across the floor, covered in dust, and damp. The last owner had run out of money, and it was in dire need of a very good architect with a very keen eye.

That was where I came in.

It was a project. Just not one *I* alone was contracted for.

"Hello?" I heard a familiar voice call out. "Tom, is that you?"

Grinning, I made my way to the front door. Cooper was standing there, looking handsome as ever, but extremely confused.

"What's going on?" he asked. "Louisa told me I had an appointment booked for a new contract. Said I was to meet the guy on site, but when I got here, your car was out front..." His words trailed off. I thought the penny had just dropped. "Tom, what are you doing?"

"I wanted you to see this place," I said. "I spoke to Louisa and told her I wanted the very best architect she had."

Cooper looked around the construction site I was standing in. He was still in the doorway. "Um..."

"Come in, I want to show you around."

He stepped inside. "Tom, what is this place?"

"A dump at the moment," I said honestly. "But I was thinking a collab between Arlington, meaning you, and Thomas Elkin Architecture, meaning me."

"A collaboration?" he said, still looking around, taking in the ceiling and windows. "Between you and me?"

I nodded. "Yes. I thought it was something I would do on my own, but the more I thought about it, the more I wanted your input."

"Tom... who owns this?"

I smiled. "A woman who ran out of money."

"Then what are you doing here?" he asked. "If she's not remodeling it..."

"I want to buy it," I said. "But I wanted your opinion."

Cooper's mouth fell open. "Buy it?"

I nodded. "Do you remember when we were at the Casa and you said that house wasn't the Tom you knew? It was too big, too cold and distant?"

He nodded warily. "Yeah?"

"I want this to be the Tom you know."

He blinked, twice. "You want me to design it? What for? Are you selling the apartment? Are you moving? What are you doing?"

"Come through here," I said, and he followed me into one of the rooms. There was a mantel amongst the mess, and on top of it, a rolled-up blueprint. "I want this to be ours. *We'll* still have the apartment because that's where *we* live. And no, *we're* not moving. But this place... well, this place will just be ours. Where we come to get away, to spend time alone, for weekends."

I took a nervous breath and handed him the tightly rolled blueprint plan.

And waited.

Cooper slid the metal band from the plans and unrolled them. He looked over the plans, which were basically blank. I saw the confusion on his face, then he realized he was still holding the metal band in his hand.

He looked at it.

Then at me, then back to the silver ring in the palm of his hand.

I saw the rapid rise and fall of his chest. I swear I could

hear his mind racing, and when he looked up at me, I saw it in his eyes.

He knew what it was. He swallowed thickly. "Tom?"

I smiled. "You know what a sense of place is?"

Cooper nodded. "It's when the place you're in feels like home. Where you're at peace."

I nodded. "That's exactly right."

Cooper looked around. "This place?"

I shook my head. "No."

His voice kind of squeaked. "Me?"

I nodded and grinned. "You're my sense of place, Cooper."

He looked back at the ring he was still holding.

"Marry me," I said. "Build me a house that's made of us, that reminds you of who we are."

Cooper bit his lip, and his eyes welled with tears. Then he nodded.

"Yes?"

He nodded again. "Yes."

"Did I ask right this time?"

He nodded, then the first of his tears fell. "Yes."

I wrapped my arms around him and he held onto me so tight and buried his face into my neck. "Did you want to see the rest of the house?"

He nodded but didn't move to let me go. Eventually he pulled back and handed me the ring. Before I could ask, he said, "You have to put it on my finger. You need to do it properly."

I took the silver ring, then his left hand, and slid the ring over his finger. He took my face in his hands and kissed me tenderly. "I'm so in love with you," he whispered. Then he wiped his face and laughed before he took my hand. "Come on, show me the rest of the house."

He led me through each room—granted, there weren't many of them—and I could see his excitement grow with each new discovery. I could also tell he was mapping out and planning, seeing visions in his head.

"How am I supposed to go back to work now?" he asked, as I locked the front door behind us. "I'm too excited!"

"You have a lot to plan," I said, kissing him at the Arlington company car. "You need to tell Louisa you'll be doing your first joint account."

"What are you doing?" he asked.

"I need to drop off the key back at the real estate office and sign some papers. I'll need to call my lawyer and my accountant," I said. I was playing with his left hand, turning the ring around his finger. "I'll have some papers for you to sign as well."

"Prenup?" he asked. "I have no problem with that."

I laughed. "No, silly. Papers to sign for the purchase of this place. It will be in both our names."

"Tom, I... I can't afford it—"

I kissed him quiet. "I don't care. This place is ours." Then I told him, "And you'll need to think of a name. It doesn't have one currently. The old owners never called it anything."

Cooper exhaled through puffed cheeks and took another deep breath. He looked at the ring on his finger and touched it, then he looked back to me. There was a humbled softness in his eyes. "How did I ever get so lucky?"

I kissed him again. "I often ask myself the same question." He held onto me and kissed me deeply, and when he pulled his mouth away, he left his forehead pressed to mine. "Drive safely," I said. "I'll see you at home tonight."

I'D ONLY BEEN home for a short while, sitting on the sofa, looking through some legal papers, when I heard the familiar sound of Cooper's keys in the door. He came through the door like there was a demon behind him and never took his eyes off me.

"You're home early," I said.

"I couldn't wait," he replied. "I couldn't concentrate and I was bouncing in my seat, apparently. Louisa told me to go home."

Without another word, he took the papers from my hand and put them on the coffee table, took my hand, and led me to our bedroom.

"Uh, Cooper," I said with a laugh.

He didn't answer me until we were next to the bed, when he turned to face me. There was a look of love, a little fear, and a lot of determination on his face. "I said I couldn't wait," he whispered.

"Cooper, what is it?"

"I want you," he said softly. "I want you to have me... bare."

My eyes widened. "Cooper..."

"You don't have to if you're not ready," he said quickly. "I probably should have asked first. But I have this feeling, this need, that if you don't do it, I think I'll die."

I would've laughed if he wasn't so serious. I put my hands to his face. "Are you okay?"

"I've never been better," he replied. "Just today has been so much emotion, and I can't seem to contain it. I can't... I'm not making much sense."

I kissed him then, softly, deeply, and started to undress

him. I knew exactly what he meant. "You're making perfect sense."

There was a desperation in his touch, in his kiss, and when we were both naked on the bed, I took the lube but left the condoms in the bedside table. "Are you sure?" I asked one final time.

He nodded. "Yes."

I knelt between his spread thighs, prepping him while I kissed over his chest, his jaw, his neck. He was so desperate, panting and pleading, with frantic fingers and grinding hips. When he was ready for me, I leaned over him as I pressed the head of my cock against his hole. He held my face as I pushed inside him.

"Oh my God," I mumbled. It felt so good, so real. I slowly slid all the way inside him, giving us both time to adjust. When he lifted his hips and thrust against me, I cried out, "Slow. Please, baby, slow."

His eyes were wide and he brought my face to his, kissing me passionately. I tried to rein in my body's desire to fuck hard, but it was getting to be too much.

I leaned back, resting my weight on one hand, and took his cock in my other hand. He batted my hand away and started to pull himself while I thrust slowly into him. "I need you to come first," I said with a groan. "Please, come for me."

A few more strokes of his hand and his body went rigid beneath me, his head pushed back, and he groaned as stripes of come lined his stomach. I couldn't wait any longer. I thrust into him, deep and hard, making his eyes pop open, and he cried out in pleasure as my cock swelled and emptied inside him. Like my body splintered into a thousand pieces, and he held me together while I surged inside him.

"Oh, Tom," he murmured, over and over. I buried my face into his neck, and he held me so tight. When I finally moved to pull out of him, he stopped me. "Stay inside me," he whispered and kissed my neck, my shoulder. "I never want you to leave."

I could barely form a coherent thought, but I managed to tell him I never would.

TWO YEARS LATER

I TURNED INTO THE DRIVE, and like every time I saw it, I smiled when I saw the name on the gate. 'Winston' was the name Cooper had given this place. He'd wanted to name it after me, but I'd told him it should reflect him too. So then he'd wanted the name of the cottage to somehow reflect some translation of 'sense of place' and I'd told him maybe he was over-thinking it.

Then he'd thrown his arms up and yelled at me. "At this fucking rate, I may as well call it Gary or Ian, or fucking Winston!"

Well, we had dropped the 'fucking' prefix but kept the Winston.

No matter what we called it, it was home.

During the course of construction, Cooper would bring something home, be it a small floor rug or a frame for the wall, and when I'd ask him who it was for, he'd smile and answer, "Winston."

It was like the small cottage became a living entity, another person, and in many ways, I guess it did. Winston was a huge part of our lives.

Even if we only spent every other weekend there, or any vacations we could, it was home. Sometimes, when work allowed, we'd base ourselves there. It was serene, peaceful—it was a part of us. I'd asked Cooper to design it, to decorate it, so it was indicative of both of us, and he'd done it well.

It was a place that, as soon as you walked through the front door, you felt at ease. It was like pulling on an old favorite pair of jeans or a favorite sweater. It was comfort, it was familiar, and it was... home.

Just as he'd said it should be, it was now warm timbers, slate floors, rugs, and rustic stonework. Books, plans, and maps adorned the walls. It was perfect.

I pulled my car in behind Cooper's. He'd driven up earlier today, saying he could work from home while I had some meetings in the City, and I told him I'd meet him here.

I walked in, taking in the familiar smell and the warmth of the fire, and headed straight for Cooper's favorite room, knowing that was where I'd find him.

He turned from his drafting board and smiled at me as I walked in. "Hey, you."

"Hey, handsome," I replied, kissing him softly. He had on a sweater and jeans and was looking particularly comfortable.

He sighed contentedly and looked up at me. "You ready for tomorrow?"

"I am so ready," I said, taking off my glasses. A testament to my age and too much time looking at computer screens, my failing eyesight now required glasses. I was almost afraid to show him, but Cooper loved them on me.

Cooper took the glasses from me, folded them, and rested them on the lip of his drafting board. "Sofia called," he said. "Mom, Dad and Max are on their way."

I smiled and kissed the top of his head. "Ryan and

Bianca are driving up after work," I said. "And Jennifer will be here in the morning."

Cooper smiled again. "Isn't it against tradition for us to see each other in the morning?"

I kissed him softly. "I don't care much for tradition."

We were having a small ceremony here at the cabin. Our guests, who consisted mostly of family, were staying at the Casa, thanks to Sofia's generous offer. Everyone had pretty much organized the entire thing for us, including the catering and decorations. All Cooper and I basically had to do was be here.

"I can't wait to marry you," he said reverently. "I wish it was happening today."

"You're so impatient," I said with a smile.

"It's a Gen Y thing, remember?"

"How could I ever forget?"

"Did you remember the rings?" he asked.

I resisted rolling my eyes. I pulled a small box out of my pocket. "Want to see them?"

Cooper's eyes lit up and he nodded. So I opened the box for him, and he took out both metal bands. He'd picked them out, but we'd needed them resized, so I'd added a surprise engraving. I waited for him to notice it, then he looked at me.

Written inside both bands were three words.

"*Et cor domum*," I murmured. "It's what you are to me."

His eyes darted to mine. "What does that mean?"

"It's Latin," I murmured. "It means 'heart and home.'"

Cooper's eyes softened and he smiled, almost tearful. "Oh, Tom. It's perfect. That's what you are, that's exactly what you are."

I leaned down and kissed him softly. "Heart and home."

"Always."

EPILOGUE

Four Years Later

Cooper

I SAT IN MY OFFICE, staring out of the window. I'd been at Arlington Initiative for six years, and I was as happy there now as I had been the day I'd started. I had my own office, got my own jobs, secured my own contracts, and had complete control from the first meeting until construction completion. Tom kept asking me to quit so we could work together, but I was happy where I was. I saw how much he loved being his own boss, but I told him until such a time when Arlington impeded on my creativity and stopped encouraging me to flourish, then I'd forgo branching out on my own with the added stress of being self-employed.

My email pinged on my laptop, and I saw it was from my boss, Louisa.

I smiled as I opened it, and when I read the words *vacation time approved*, I turned to the glass wall that fronted the main office area and found her grinning back at me.

Without wasting a second, I opened my Internet browser and began my search at the same time that I called the only person on the planet who could help me. "Hi, Jennifer. It's Cooper. Listen, I need your help."

Tom had been avoiding any discussions about his birthday. He wanted no part of it—he wanted no party, no celebration, and certainly no reminders.

Turning fifty was hitting him hard.

It was so unlike him to be bothered by a number. I knew he'd had his freak-out before he'd turned forty, but that was for a different reason. He'd needed to stop living a lie, he'd needed to come out before he'd turned forty—or so he'd convinced himself. But maybe the problem was that I was still in my twenties. I was twenty-eight. The twenty-two-year age gap between us would never change, but something in his head told him being fifty while his husband was in his twenties made him... old.

The fact that some waiter at a restaurant last week had assumed I was his son didn't help matters either. I'd laughed it off, but it had really bothered Tom. And his impending birthday, his dreaded fiftieth, loomed over him like a dark cloud.

That's why I needed to make his gift special.

I needed to remind him that I loved him when he was twenty-two years older than me when we got married, and I loved him still when he was twenty-two years older than me today.

I needed to find the perfect gift. One that would show him exactly how I felt, exactly what he meant to me. I needed to show him that the age difference between us was what made us work. So, with that in mind, I let my mind wander...

Tom.

Love.

Timeless.

Architecture.

The perfect retrofit.

An absolute sense of place.

I smiled and searched for the most perfect gift.

TWO WEEKS LATER, against Tom's wishes, I held a small party for him at our apartment. He'd tried to argue with me—seriously, he should have known better by now—but to relent a little, I invited strictly family and closest friends only.

There were about twenty people in all, including Ryan and Bianca, Sofia and her new husband, Phil, and Jennifer and her husband of thirty years.

I'd hired wait staff to serve food and drinks, so all I had to do was entertain and be awesome. Truly, I didn't even have to try. Tom, on the other hand, was struggling.

"Can you try to smile?" I asked him gently. We finally had a moment alone near the kitchen. I put my arm around his waist and gave him a squeeze. "The birthday boy is supposed to be happy."

"I am," he said. "It's just... I didn't want a fuss."

"This isn't a fuss." I looked around at our guests, all of whom were chatting and laughing. "Me paying the City to stop traffic in Times Square so we could waltz in the middle of the street in front of the world's media would be me making a fuss."

He groaned painfully and downed his champagne. "You wouldn't."

"No," I admitted cheerfully. "But just so you know, my thirtieth is in a year and a half, and if you can't think of any ideas..."

At least that made him smile. For a moment. Then he frowned.

Shit. I had to mention my age, didn't I?

Just then Sofia came up to us. "Is something the matter?" she asked quietly.

I shouldn't have been surprised that she could tell. They'd been married for twenty-something years and were now back to being close friends.

I sighed and spoke for him. "He says he's fine, but this whole turning-fifty thing is stressing him out. He hasn't said as much, but he doesn't like the idea of being in his fifties while I'm—" I cringed. "—not quite thirty."

Tom stared at me.

I eyeballed him. "Tell me I'm wrong."

Tom made a face and looked away.

"See? I'm never wrong," I said to Sofia. "Can you tell him he's being ridiculous, please?"

Sofia pursed her lips. "No, I won't."

Wait, what? No?

Tom looked at her, his whole face indignant.

Sofia pointed a well-manicured finger at his chest. "You're not being ridiculous, Tom. You're being selfish, rude, and disrespectful to Cooper."

Oh.

She wasn't finished. "Tom, I love you dearly. But you need to get over yourself. He loved you then; he loves you now. You'd think after fifty years you'd have learned not to waste a minute, yes?"

I could have hugged her. Then I thought, *fuck it*, so I did hug her. Then I hugged Tom. "I can see why you married her," I said, thinking that would finally make him laugh.

It didn't. "I'm starting to think I must like being bossed around," he replied with a smile that didn't quite work.

"Tom, what's really wrong?" I asked. Maybe it was the look on my face, maybe he could tell how scared I suddenly was. Maybe it was how my voice was quiet or the look in my eyes. This was not the place I would have chosen to have this conversation, not at his birthday party, but something wasn't right. "Please?"

Tom swallowed hard and stared at me. "Do you remember Robert Chandler?"

I nodded. "He was the prick who tried to get you fired from Brackett and Golding."

"He had a stroke two weeks ago," Tom said quietly. "He's bed-ridden, needs around-the-clock care..."

I shook my head. *No, no, no. Just no.* "Tom, you listen to me. You're fit, healthy. You're not like him."

"My father had a stroke," he whispered.

Oh, fuck. How did I miss the connection?

"Oh, Tom," Sofia whispered.

He was still staring at me. "What if I...? I can't expect you to... You're only twenty-eight."

My heart literally fell through the floor. Yes, we were standing away from the crowd, but we were still at a party. In our living room. Surrounded by our nearest and dearest. I wanted to cry. I wanted to scream and punch something. Instead, I took a deep breath and spoke as quietly as I could. "Tom, do you remember when we got married, and I said in sickness and in health?"

He balked.

"You remember that, right? Because I do. I said it because I meant it. Do you know what it does to me when you tell me it didn't mean anything to you? That you'd think so little of me as to assume I wouldn't care for you?"

"Oh, no," he said, shaking his head. His eyes were wide and filled with remorse and fear. "That's not what I meant at all."

"Because you have to believe me when I say this, Tom, it fucking hurts that you would think that."

He threw his arms around me and pulled me in tight. My face was buried in his neck. "No, Cooper, my love. That's not what I meant. I'm sorry."

"You should be," I told him. I pulled back so he could see my face. "There was no fine print, Tom. There was no subclause to revoke vows because one of us might get sick. Do you under-fucking-stand me?"

He nodded.

"Do you need me to write down a definition of forever, you know, with your Alzheimer's and all."

Sofia snorted a teary laugh beside us. I'd forgotten she was there, and this time when Tom smiled, it was genuine. "I love you," he said to me. "Sometimes I forget just how much you love me in return."

I looked at Sofia. "See? Alzheimer's. He forgets all the important stuff." Then I gave him a quick kiss. "I love you too. Next time, please talk to me. Or Sofia. Or Jennifer, or Ryan. Okay?"

He nodded again but looked like the weight of the world was off his shoulders. When I finally let go of him, Sofia kissed his cheek. "Happy birthday, Tom," she said, walking back to Phil with a smile.

Tom put his hand on my waist and pulled me against him. This time we danced. Like we'd done countless times in our living room when it was just us, slow and sensual. Normally this kind of dancing ended in bed or with an epic make-out session on the sofa that normally ended in bed. And it wasn't long before the other guests noticed us in the corner, slow dancing and soft kissing.

So I grabbed his hand and led him to the table where the gifts were and asked for everyone's attention. "First of all, I'd like to thank you all for coming. It means a great deal to both of us," I said. "Tom, very adamantly, didn't want any speeches. He also told you all not to bring any gifts, and the fact that you all still did just shows what impeccable taste in friends he has.

"Now, I'm allowed to break the no-speech rule because, well, because I never do anything he tells me to do anyway."

"It's true," Tom said. He was blushing and looking all sorts of handsome.

In fact, his shy smile and nervous lip-bite made me lose my train of thought completely. "Um... What was I saying?"

Everyone laughed, and of course that only embarrassed Tom some more.

"Right," I said with a chuckle. I put one arm around his waist and continued. "I was telling you all about this wonderful man I married who, despite not wanting to turn fifty, is the smartest, most brilliant, sexiest damn fifty-year-old I know." I raised my champagne glass and made a toast. "To Tom."

Everyone raised their glass and repeated my toast and, rather reluctantly, Tom decided to respond. He'd gone from looking shy to resigned, and even a bit sad. "It's true," he started. "I didn't want to turn fifty. I guess saying you're in your forties is still kinda young, but..." He shrugged. "Saying you're in your fifties isn't. But then tonight I was reminded by someone younger and wiser than me"—he looked squarely at me—"of what love really is. Of what life really is. And I'm truly grateful. For everyone here. For everything."

After everyone had toasted once more, I couldn't wait anymore. I handed him his gift. It was a rectangular box and the noise it made kind of gave it away, but he grinned anyway. Whereas I would have just torn at the paper, Tom slid his finger under the tape and unwrapped it delicately to reveal the box of Lego.

Those who knew us knew the significance. Our little cottage in the Hamptons had a cabinet of a few Lego-built buildings from their architectural range, from all the places we'd been together. It had started with the Sydney Opera House and now included the Flatiron Building, the Lincoln Memorial, and the Seattle Space Needle.

This particular one was the Eiffel Tower.

Tom tilted his head. "We haven't been there," he said, clearly confused.

"Look in the box," I told him.

He hadn't even noticed that the Lego box had been opened. But his eyes went wide when he pulled out the envelope with a flight itinerary on it. "Paris?"

I nodded. "Two tickets, a tour of the Eiffel Tower and a private showing of the Rudy Ricciotti exhibition at the Cité de l'Architecture et du Patrimoine," I said, no doubt butchering the French language.

Everyone awwwed at the gift, but it was only Tom who really got the significance. I knew he would. I had no doubt.

He got a bit teary. "Are you trying to tell me something?"

I nodded. "I knew you'd get it. I thought you might need reminding."

"Get what?" Ryan asked. "Reminding of what?"

Tom read over the itinerary and his grin grew wider and his eyes got even tearier. "The Louvre, the Eiffel Tower, and Rudy Ricciotti's work are just three of the world's best examples of retrofit. Where the new and old meet, complement and enhance. Both generations of design contribute equally to make each structure what it is."

I nodded. He got it.

"How did you get all that from *that*?" Ryan asked, clearly oblivious to the elements of architecture and how they related to his father and me.

"Because I did need reminding. And because Cooper knows me better than I know myself."

I nodded. "It's true. I do."

Tom pulled me in for a warm embrace. "And I'll never forget it again. I promise," he whispered in my ear.

"Good," I replied. "But don't worry. I'll always remind you."

He laughed. "Thank you."

"And when we're in Paris," I added, "we might want to get some inspiration for our first public Elkin-Jones design."

He pulled back, his eyes wide. "Serious?"

"Don't get too excited. I'm not leaving Arlington, but I think it's time we let the world see what we can do together."

Tom smiled like I'd never seen him smile before. "You really are kind of awesome."

I rolled my eyes. "For the love of God, Tom. I've been telling you that for six years."

Our friends, all still gathered around us, laughed. Tom raised his champagne glass. "A toast to the last fifty years." He smiled right at me. "And may the next fifty be just as blessed."

I clinked my glass to his. "I'll drink to that."

The End

SENSE OF PLACE
N.R. WALKER

THE THOMAS ELKIN SERIES

ABOUT THE AUTHOR

N.R. Walker is an Australian author, who loves her genre of
gay romance.
She loves writing and spends far too much time doing it but
wouldn't have it any other way.

She is many things: a mother, a wife, a sister, a writer. She
has pretty, pretty boys who live in her head, who don't let
her sleep at night unless she gives them life with words.

She likes it when they do dirty, dirty things... but likes it
even more when they fall in love.

She used to think having people in her head talking to her
was weird, until one day she happened across other writers
who told her it was normal.

She's been writing ever since...

Contact the author
nrwalker.net
nrwalker@nrwalker.net

ALSO BY N.R. WALKER

Blind Faith

Through These Eyes (Blind Faith #2)

Blindside: Mark's Story (Blind Faith #3)

Ten in the Bin

Point of No Return – Turning Point #1

Breaking Point – Turning Point #2

Starting Point – Turning Point #3

Element of Retrofit – Thomas Elkin Series #1

Clarity of Lines – Thomas Elkin Series #2

Sense of Place – Thomas Elkin Series #3

Taxes and TARDIS

Three's Company

Red Dirt Heart

Red Dirt Heart 2

Red Dirt Heart 3

Red Dirt Heart 4

Red Dirt Christmas

Cronin's Key

Cronin's Key II

Cronin's Key III

Exchange of Hearts

The Spencer Cohen Series, Book One

The Spencer Cohen Series, Book Two

The Spencer Cohen Series, Book Three

The Spencer Cohen Series, Yanni's Story

Blood & Milk

The Weight Of It All

A Very Henry Christmas (The Weight of It All 1.5)

Perfect Catch

Switched

Imago

Imagines

Red Dirt Heart Imago

On Davis Row

Free Reads

Sixty Five Hours

Learning to Feel

His Grandfather's Watch (And The Story of Billy and Hale)

The Twelfth of Never (Blind Faith 3.5)

Twelve Days of Christmas (Sixty Five Hours Christmas)

Best of Both Worlds

Translated Titles

Fiducia Cieca (Italian translation of Blind Faith)

Attraverso Questi Occhi (Italian translation of Through These Eyes)

Preso alla Sprovvista (Italian translation of Blindside)

Il giorno del Mai (Italian translation of Blind Faith 3.5)

Cuore di Terra Rossa (Italian translation of Red Dirt Heart)

Cuore di Terra Rossa 2 (Italian translation of Red Dirt Heart 2)

Cuore di Terra Rossa 3 (Italian translation of Red Dirt Heart 3)

Natale di terra rossa (Terra rossa 3.5)

Cuore di Terra Rossa 4 (Italian translation of Red Dirt Heart 4)

Confiance Aveugle (French translation of Blind Faith)

A travers ces yeux: Confiance Aveugle 2 (French translation of Through These Eyes)

Aveugle: Confiance Aveugle 3 (French translation of Blindside)

À Jamais (French translation of Blind Faith 3.5)

Cronin's Key (French translation)

Cronin's Key II (French translation)

Au Coeur de Sutton Station (French translation of Red Dirt Heart)

Partir ou rester (French translation of Red Dirt Heart 2)

Faire Face (French translation of Red Dirt Heart 3)

Trouver sa place (French translation of Red Dirt Heart 4)

Rote Erde (German translation of Red Dirt Heart)

Rote Erde 2 (German translation of Red Dirt Heart 2)